The Valley of the Still Waters

J.R. Roberts

The Valley of the Still Waters

Before we were ever born our stories began; they will continue even when our names on the stones fade from lack of remembrance......

"What are we going to do?" Juanita was beside herself from over hearing her parents talking about a possible marriage arrangement.

"I don't know! How about we just disappear tonight? Leave Texas and go West," Antonio was still in shock of the news.

"Can we?" With tear filled eyes, she firmly grasped both his arms.

"What will your father say?" Juanita was thinking of Antonio and his relationship to his family. They were a close family.

"I think that he would want me to follow my heart."

The Sanchez family had always lived in Waco even before it was in the State of Texas. The Estavan Sanchez family worked a small farm, raising some cattle, horses and cotton. For all accounts they just managed to earn a living. The family was a happy one even though they had few material things, their wealth was in family relationships.

They spent a lovers' time underneath the Texas Live oaks on the bank of the Brazos. Not wanting to go but they had to in order to prepare for their escape; a journey into the unknown but together. They gathered up the ground cloth and picnic basket. Antonio helped Juanita onto her horse. He patted the back of her boot, securing it in the stirrup.

"Go home and pack; I will do the same, it will be getting dark soon. We'll meet at the bridge when the moon is at its highest. Everything will be okay; we'll be together." She leaned down and with his left hand he stroked her face and kissed her once more. They both left to do what their hearts told them to do.

Upon arriving, she asked the ranch hand to care for her horse. She left orders to rub down her horse and place a fresh saddle blanket when he saddled him tonight. A second horse was to be saddled with a traveling rig containing supplies. She immediately went upstairs to bathe and pack.

"Juanita," Her mother came into the bedroom without knocking.

"Your father has been asking for you. He is in the parlor. Don't keep him waiting; he has some news for you."

"There you are; I have been waiting for you. No doubt you have been with the Sanchez boy again. I've asked you not to encourage him. HE is not your station. No need to mix words here. I have decided that it is time that you marry."

"What?" Juanita was even more shocked by the news as her dad confirmed what she had overheard.

"What about Nora or Dee? They are older than me."

"I have not found a suitable match for them." He was opening drawers in his desk searching for papers.

"I have found one for you. He is going to California, his family owns land and a large ranch there."

I don't want to get married; I don't want to marry a stranger. I want to marry the one I choose." These word had obviously feel onto deaf ears.

"The arrangements have been made. This is my decision. Discussion is over. You will be married and that's that." His tone was not of a loving father. It was more like a boss to a hired hand. He had made a business transaction and had sold her hand to the highest bidder. With the news confirmed, she quickly left the parlor. She packed only riding clothing. She stayed upstairs, waiting until the appointed time to meet Antonio. After packing, she just couldn't leave with saying goodbye, so she wrote a letter explaining her reasons for doing this.

Juanita's mother met her at the bedroom door, "Juana, why are your bags packed?"

As the moon rose, Antonio was already there waiting for her. When the moon was at its peak, he became anxious for the arrival of Juanita. He rode part way across the bridge to wait for her. When he heard the horses approach, he was relieved. As the horses move toward him the moonlight revealed its riders. It was Senor Ramos and the lead foremen.

"Boy, I was young once, and I remember what it was like to have someone waiting. I've come to tell you that she will not be going with you anywhere. She will be married by the weeks end. You are not to see her again. I've been patient long enough. If you don't leave this alone, I will make sure that your family is homeless. I own that farm they are working. This is a family matter, and you're not going to be family. I've chosen someone for her who has a future."

Antonio wanted to disrespect the wishes of the Ramos family. He wanted what his heart wanted but he didn't want his family to suffer. He went to Juanita's house to see if he could visit with her.   He went to her window to see if she was there, just like he has always done. She was not in her room this night.

The Ramos family had moved from Mexico City, Mexico, where Concepcion Ramos had been an architect. He was hired to help with the building of the Suspension Bridge across the Brazos River. He had business and political plans after the completion of the project.

The project allowed the Chisholm Trail to go straight through Waco, Texas. At the conclusion of the bridge project, he was hired by the Northwestern Railroad. The Ramos family consisted of Andreas, the wife; and their children Nora (18), Dee (16), and Juanita (15). The Ramos family had wealth and prestige.

What could he offer Juanita? Only Love. Antonio left that night. He left his family and his love. He faced reality; he took with him memories of his family and heartache. In the end he let his head overcome his heart, a decision that he would regret for the rest of his life. He headed east instead of going west to the Indian Territory.

The wedding took place, and as planned, the newly-married couple boarded a train heading for California to start their new lives. She left her family and love. She faced reality; she took with her memories of her family and the unanswered question as to why he did not come for her.

(Silver City, New Mexico 1873)
Several weeks later, Antonio had made his

way to Silver City, New Mexico. With the discovery of silver ore in the hills of Chloride Flats west of the farm of Captain John Bullard in the 60's, prospectors poured in, changing the once quiet Apache campsite into a silver boom town. The town of Silver City was born on 1870. Captain Bullard laid out the town's streets but never saw the town grow. He was killed in a conflict with Apace raiders.

Tony had never seen such an event, with men waging money on the outcome, saloon girls busying themselves bringing drinks to tables, and all the while the two men exchanging blows for money. Tony watched from the bar until the fair-haired boy got the best of his opponent. The fight ended as soon as the shorter man hit the floor, unconscious, and the right hand of the victor was raised.

Men collected their earnings and went back to their drinking. The unconscious fighter sat recovering sitting with friends telling what he did wrong. The victor came to the bar to buy drinks for his friends, bloodied and smiling just the same. He turned to Tony and asked, "Buy you a drink?"

"How about I buy you one? You put on a good fight," Tony said.

"It was a lucky punch. I'd take them anytime. Where are my manners? My name is Tom, Tom Lee, glad to meet you." His hand was extended, waiting for Tony to shake it.

"My name is Tony Sanchez. Glad to meet you, too." Tony reached out and shook his hand.

"Slim, how's about a couple of drinks down here," Tom yelled out to the bar keeper.

"What'll it be Tom, the usual?" Joseph Slim Roberts was the owner/operator of the Silver Cards Gambling Hall and the Silver City Freighting Company.

"Of course, make that two, one for my friend here." Tom got the first round of drinks.

"Okay, two beers coming up on the house." Slim was a man of little words, but what he said, he meant. With Tom's winning tonight's fight, Slim made some money on side bets.

"Well, Tony Sanchez, I haven't seen you in town before," Tom said.

"I am passing through to the Indian Territory."

"Is there gold or silver there?" Tom assumed Tony was a prospector.

"I don't know, I not a prospector."

"What do you do, if you don't mind me asking?" Tom asked.

"I was raised on a farm, but I am willing to do anything." Tony was about out of money. "What about you? What do you do when you're not fighting?"

"Whatever I can find; anything that I can do from my horse. I tried prospecting, but it was not the life for me. I want to earn a living off my horse instead of my back." Tom downed his beer and waved for more.

"How about these prizes fights you do?" Tony asked.

"That hurts more than the mining," said Tom, rubbing his jaw.

"What's in the Indian Territory?" he asked.

"Opportunity," Tony replied.

"I think I'm through here. How about you and I travel to the Indian Territory and see if we can make a go of it? It beats riding alone, right?" Tom asked, still rubbing his jaw.

"It sounds good to me. I plan on leaving in the morning. Enough time for you to gather your things Tom?"

"I'll be ready." Tom smiled and they both shook hands.

"Meet me for breakfast, on me, and then we can leave. Hate leaving on an empty stomach." Tom took another drink. It didn't take very long for the two to strike up a partnership and a friendship.

They traveled eastward to the Indian Territory without incident. Within weeks, they were the best of friends. Tom and Tony were about the same age, with Tom being the more outgoing and Tony the more reserved.

A month later, they found themselves in the town of The Valley of the Still Waters. The first order of business was to have supper at the only cafe in town. After being seated at a table near the front so they could see who was coming in, they ordered supper.

As the sun was setting, a diminutive figure entered the front door of the cafe with the last rays of sunlight casting a silhouette across the floor. With mouths full, both stopped chewing to gaze at the young lady. Tom was smitten by her. Tony admired her beauty, but his heart was with someone else. After the doors shut, her features could be seen clearly. Her parents were already seated next to the men. For the rest of their meal, they tried not to get caught looking at her. Every now and again, they were caught looking which brought smiles to all except Tony who was embarrassed.

After supper the men waited outside, hoping that she would pass and they would get one last look. They waited for 30 minutes until they got their chance. She waited with her mom and sister until her father retrieved the carriage from the livery stable.

She turned toward Antonio and Tom, who were trying to be inconspicuous, and said "Hello."

Tony dropped his head when the rush of blood came to his face and uttered something inaudible, Tom filled the awkward time and said, "Hello my name is Tom Lee and this is my best friend Tony Sanchez." Tom was patting him on the back and moving forward whilst Tony kept his head down.

"My name is Meagan Morgan, but everyone calls me Meg."

"Your friend is awfully shy, isn't he?" Meg bent down some to get a better look at Tony's face.

"He's just quiet," Tom countered. Tony was glad to see the carriage pull up so the awkwardness of the moment would end.

"Good-bye Tom. Tony, I hope to see you around." As the carriage left, Meg looked back. She waved good-bye, looking at Tony. It took everything he had to wave back.

Tony, my boy, I think this town has some possibilities, and I do believe you just missed yours," said Tom smiling even wider and patting Tony even harder.

"Really, it has nothing to do with Megan? Tony jabbed Tom' ribs with his elbow. "And I believe she was waving at me?" As Tony continuing to jab Tom.

"Maybe. Come on; let's see what kind of work we can find. I think she's the kind that needs to be courted properly." The two left, joking about what just happened. It was in no time that they both found work on an outlying ranch.

{The Napa Valley- California wine country}

Carlos worked the slaughter houses of South San Francisco ever since he came to California. His Tio Julio needed him on the ranch, but Carlos wanted to live in a big city.

His mother was still in Arizona, and he wanted her to move to California. Juanita wanted nothing to do with her mother-in-law. It was bad enough to have your parents just give you away. But to think that you would have to put up with the mother-in-law, too!

As time passed, everything was as good as an arranged marriage could be. To this day, Juanita could not love him. Her heart was with the one that she left behind. Through the years she settled into the marriage and made peace with her life. She never forgot him, and to this day she kept the secret.

Carlos met with, Alonzo Della Francesca, a wine grower, and started to ask questions about the vineyards and the workings of the wine industry. The industry was in its infancy in California. He invited Carlos to bring some men and work for a time during the harvest to learn more about the process of grape cutting and harvesting and, ultimately, the business of the vineyard.

Carlos, always the entrepreneur, saw the opportunity he was waiting for. This was a way to make money and find work for others. He took Mr. Francesca up on his offer and proceeded to find men to work the vineyards.

Many seasons passed. Carlos had learned enough of the wine industry to know he wanted to own a vineyard of his own. Jesse had grown-up and was working alongside his father. He liked being next to his father except for the times his father was intoxicated. They worked tirelessly to make the most of their time in the vineyards. Jesse loved the mountains and decided that he, too, would someday own a vineyard.

While in the fields working, Carlos was a different man. He was generous with his words when his children were working beside him. He watched over them, making sure that each had what was needed for the day. He would direct questions toward them, genuinely interested in each. Only in this setting did he seem interested in what they had to say. The children wanted to work all day just to feel like they mattered.

Mr. Francesca took a special interest in Jesse and gave him a more comprehensive look into the production of the wines. Jesse showed promise in becoming a connoisseur of the wines and his understanding of the distillation processes allowed him to assist in the making of brandies.

He loved it all; hybridizing new stock plants, making new varieties of grapes, harvesting the fruit, and making the products. This is what he wanted to do with his life.

"You have shown an interest in the vineyard and all that goes into the creation of the fine wines, Jesse. In the short time you have been here, you have learned a great deal. You have a passion for the art," said Mr. Francesca while he was sampling one of the aged casks of brandies. He offered Jesse some of the brandy to taste and to give his opinion.

"Thank you, sir."

"Have you thought of going to the university to learn more?" Mr. Francesca inquired.

"I have not thought about it, Mr. Francesca," Jesse replied.

"Think about it. I can use someone who has the same passion as I do."

"Yes sir, I will think about it, and thank you." Jesse tipped his hat to Mr. Francesca.

Tio Julio telegraphed Carlos and extended yet another invitation for them to move down to the San Joaquin Valley and help with the ranch. This time wasting little time the family relocated to the ranch. It was the right thing to do. Carlos still had the dream of owning his own vineyard, but his uncle needed him more. The town of Senora de la Merced, for now will be home for the De La Souza family.

Juanita wanted to get back to more

comfortable surroundings so the children could grow and learn values not learned in the city. For the next few years there was much happiness and the family grew. There is nothing like being around family and it was good to see them content.

Carlos inherited the ranch after the death of his uncle and later acquired the neighboring ranches after their owners could not make a go of it. It seemed that Carlos had it all wealth, prestige and respect.

Then Carlos received a telegraph that changed his life and ultimately changed the lives of all the De La Souza family forever. He learned that his mother had died. Carlos could not overcome his grief, so he started to drink even more. The self-pity turned into abuse aimed at those he loved. He was always sorry the next day, but it never was the same. The children did not understand what had become of their father. Juanita endured it. This abuse went on for years. Jesse witnessed it all, and on most occasions was at the receiving end of it. When he reached his sixteenth birthday, he was finally able to put a stop to it.

{Family ties broken}

"Why do you let him do this to us?" Jesse asked his mother.

"I will not let him get away with it anymore; I will not be treated like this! He treats strangers better, he treats complete strangers better. I've had enough. I will not be treated like this again. It ends tonight." With each remark, Jesse's throat tightened with so much hatred that he could no longer hold back tears of frustration. And with that, he left the house.

His father became irate when his children defied him. They were always made examples of for the other to see. The other children had long ago learned to hide behind doors when their father would come home drunk.

Jesse was different child. He was a strong-minded, angry young man, wanting nothing but the love of his father until now. Now all he wanted was to be left alone. He had a protective nature and would stand up to him to protect the others. He was determined to end the abuse.

The whipping would always start with a backhand to the chest. Whether it was pride or an act of defiance, Jesse would get back up and stand his ground. This insolence would enrage his father further, and the beating would go on.

Juanita could not understand why Jesse confronted his father. There were times that you were stripped of your clothing, and a small knotted, rope the size of a thumb, was used to get things under control. This time Carlos would use his fists. No one, especially the children of his home, were going to get the best of him.

As Jesse grew into his teens, he became physically powerful due to the work on the ranch and the self-defense training that Master Sheo was putting him through. Jesse's self-confidence was also growing, and so was his hatred for his father.

Juanita had no answer for the reason why this one child was so determined to fight the fight that would end badly for him. She had given up on the marriage, she just existed. The abuse had drained the life from everyone except for one.

Recently all of the abuse was being directed toward Juanita; Jesse loved his mother and was always there to help. When he was young, he witnessed the beating but could not do anything to stop them. He made the attempts, only to become a victim himself.

The next day there were apologies and empty promises to never again let his drunkenness lead to physical harm to his family. Don Carlos was usually a personal man when he was not drinking, but his drinking has caused much sorrow.

Carlos was born in Cochise County, Arizona, in the town of Cascabel near Tucson. He was raised by his mother and knew of his father only by what she had told him. He was a twin. His brother died shortly after birth. When he was a teenager, he took his mother's family name and dropped the name he was born with. Carlos met his biological father the week he left home. This man didn't deserve to have his name kept alive.

Carlos mother worked outside the home and had little time to show Carlos the love that a mother should show a fatherless child. His mother married for the 8th time, and the new husband wanted him out.

"Why do you do this to yourself? I am begging you to stop, please!" Juanita pleaded with Jesse. Those pleas were lost to anger that Jesse possessed for his father. He had finally lost the need for a relationship with his father. As far as he was concerned, his father was not his father. His resentment was just toward his father and no one else. He did not let this affect his heart and how he treated others.

{Madre De La Tierra}
With acquisition of surrounding ranches and farms, Carlos renamed the   ranch Madre De La Tierra but kept the circle DLS brand since the livestock and cattle already had the brand from his uncle. The newly-named ranch started to diversify. The new name signified what the land meant to him.   The name meant Mother Earth.

Always looking for ways to make new money, Carlos realized there was a better way to farm. The ranching portion would soon have a change, but for now, he had to find a better way to make use of the land.

Cattle and horses were not the only things they could make money from. Instead of producing the same crops every season, Carlos used a rotating crop system so vital nutrients wouldn't be exhausted. Some lands were allowed to lay fallow so they could rejuvenate. The grasslands were not only used for grazing; some were cultivated for hay. Better use of the land led to better productivity.

The farm and ranch homes were used for his foreman's homes. On one of the farms a 'campo' was built; rows of one-room houses were built on the property so his seasonal workers had decent homes for their children during the migration of seasonal harvest. The ones who stayed year-round stayed in two-bedroom houses. Why would Carlos go to all these lengths to ensure that his workers were taken care of but not do the simplest gesture to have a relationship to his own family?

Children grew up working alongside parents. Field workers were generational. Ranch work started early in the day and ended late. The children learned early that work came first; child play was left for when the work was done. Most times, it was never done.

Carlos was never to be questioned on his authority over family matters. Each De La Souza child had his or her own set of chores to do after the work day was over. This was done so that Juanita knew where the children were at all times. They were up at 5 am and in bed by dark. Life was hard on a ranch, even for the privileged. What the children didn't understand was that their parents were teaching accountability, skills, etiquette, and resilience. But affection or love was for the weak, they were nothing more than servants.

Each was in charge of his or her own horse, which meant that each took responsibility for the care of the animal. The animal was taken care of before their own needs. Carlos wanted his children to be independent yet be at his call when he needed them to carry out his demands. He wanted them to be examples to those whom he employed to see that he was the master of his house.

There were no distinctions between the girls and boys. They were all treated the same; they all worked on the ranch. Juanita treated the children the same as Carlos; she had neither daughters nor sons. Each learned to keep house and all that goes with it. Sundays was as Juanita would say, 'La Dia de Dios,' and everyone was in attendance for Mass. No excuses. Carlos spent his time on the ranch instead. For him, there was always work to be done. He attended Mass on Christmas Eve and when the Father blessed the harvest.

Carlos took the title of "Don" after he acquired the land from the local Mexican population. The term Don was a name given to the sovereign owner of the land. Carlos literally took it to mean that he was master of all, and that included his family.

{What is in a name?}
A name is of great importance. The Spanish took the choosing of names for their children seriously. A name entails all that you are. It declares your character. The family wanted the names they chose to have special significance to the children especially since they were Roman Catholic. Juanita wanted to give names to her children that indicated sense of purpose in God.

Jesse Rogelio Alano De La Souza:
Jesse-Dios esiste {God exists}
Rogelio-Famoso por su lanza {famous spear man}
Alano-El rey de todos {the king of all}
De La Souza {name originated from the Portuguese and found its way to Spain (from the town of Souza.)

Jesse was the oldest. He had dark brown hair with dark brown eyes and an olive skin color. He looked more like his mother with no likeness to his father. He had a way of making everyone around him feel at ease. Though he was withdrawn, he always had a kind word to say and was quick to help others. If the situation called for it, he would defend the weak.

Elizabeth was second after Jesse. Jesse was particularly close to her. She was outgoing and said her mind. She had a keen sense of humor and was always the one to make someone laugh. She had light brown hair and large brown eyes and was fair-skinned. She favored her mother but had her father's eyes. She was two years younger than Jesse.

Francisco had similar characteristics of his mother's uncle. He was the obedient one; always at his mother's side. Jesse was glad that he had her to watch him. He had the distinctive Spanish look. He had black hair with green eyes and rather light skin color. He was three years younger than Jesse. His features were those of his father.

Elena was the baby girl. She had dark brown eyes and an olive skin color. She always wanted to be held by Jesse. Jesse was rather fond of her. She was always getting into things and was adventurous one. She was eight years younger than Jesse.

The youngest was named Nicolas after Juanita's grandfather. He was fair skin and had light brown hair. He was to be the last of the family. There were complication at childbirth. Juanita could no longer have any more children. He was nine years younger than Jesse.

{EL Rio de Nuestra Senora de la Merced}

The San Joaquin Valley is being settled, and it was time that Merced became a town. Snelling, 26 miles to the east, was the county seat at this time. Merced because of its increasing population could replace Snelling as the county seat.

The benefit of being the county seat is that the seat can pass laws that would impact economic growth in the area. The people of the neighboring area wanted control of these issues. With the increasing population, the much needed votes to change the county seat was now in Merced's favor.

The trains were just coming into the valley. Riverboats traveled through the Merced River and Yosemite River. Bear Creek was not getting the grains and cattle down to market fast enough. It was time for a good business man to seize the opportunity to get in with the railroad and back them in all business ventures.

Don Carlos made the most of it, and purchased real estate on both sides of Bear Creek that the railroad had surveyed to use. With the land, he made concessions to the railroad, and they in turn did the same for him. The railroad surveyors told Carlos that Merced will be the official name for the new town. The town will get its name from the river that flows through it.

"El Rio de Nuestra Senora de la Merced, translates to *River of Our Lady of Mercy.* That's such a long name for a small town," the surveyor said. We at the county office abridged it, it will officially be named Merced." The town will also be known as the "Gateway to Yosemite," the route to southern California. The fur traders found it when they were searching for new fur hunting sites. The Spanish government sent the fur traders back through the pass after they were rested and given provisions. As with all things, if money was to be made men would trespass no matter the consequences.

The pass was no longer a secret. Soon fur trappers and settlers invaded the Valley. The Yosemite Valley and neighboring valleys were the worst sites of brutality ever inflicted upon the native Indians by the United States government due to the discovery of gold on Native lands.

When the Mexicans gained their independence from Spain, the area stretching from what is now southern California up to the Northern border was known as the Republic of California. Now that they had successfully gained independence, the land and its citizens no longer had the protection of Spain's army.

With Mexico having fought the war of Independence with Spain, they were in financial difficulties. Because of the size of the country, the guarding of their borders was not possible. Now that the Americans found gold in California, Mexico itself faced the threat of invasion.

{The independence of Jesse}
Carlos saw no reason for a son to speak to him in such an insolent manner. He was to be made an example of so the others would know that he is the master of his house once and for all! The tone of his voice, body posture, and the Look of

Jesse's eyes were unlike previous confrontations. Jesse looked directly into his father's eyes; he had the look of a predator looking into the eyes of prey. Jesse's stance was firm, with shoulders square and set.

Jesse's voice was calm and direct without fear; the positioning of his body almost demanded his father to engage him. Carlos had drank just enough to be drunk yet he could see that Jesses' body language was different. For the first time, Carlos was the one afraid.

Jesse stood his ground ready to defend himself. When Carlos attacked, Jesse became the aggressor; he confronted his father with a rage that he had never felt before. The confrontation was brief. Jesse was much too young and had more to gain from this fight, namely his own respect and freedom. Jesse had all the right to inflict much more damage to the man who never had much as a kind or encouraging word for him. He was the better man and ended it before he became his father.

"I will not be treated like this ever again by anyone! I will not let you treat any of us this way, or I will not stop next time!" Jesse had finally stood up to his father, but at a price. It was better to be free that to live in fear. After the fight, he was dismissed from the family and stripped of his name and his place in the De La Souza Family.

"You are not my son; you are no longer of this family!" Carlos' last hurtful words to Jesse, and they were the worst.

"No!" his mother cried.

"Mama, esta bien, I will leave." Jesse hugged his mother and told her that it was best for everyone if he did.

The words said were words that a son should not hear from a father. The meaning cut to the center of his heart. It did not matter. He had lost the respect for his father ever since he was a child and now it forced him to deal with reality. It was time that he left before this hate infected his heart and soul.

Jesse picked up his pride and left with his only belongings. He quickly packed a bag with clothing, saddled his horse and left. Because of father's influence throughout California, he looked toward the East. To become the man he knew he could be, he had to find his own way. Before he left town, he had to say good bye to Father Diego.

"Where are you going at this time of the night?" A voice came from the darkness.

The question startled Jesse, as he didn't see Father Diego in the shadows of the dimly lit sanctuary.

"It's a little late to be off riding somewhere," Father Diego said.

"I've come to ask for forgiveness, a prayer of safety for my journey, and to say good bye to you, Father." Jesse was at the altar on his knees.

"I knew this day would come. I'll give you this piece of advice. Do what is in your heart and always ask for guidance from our God. I know you, and you have a kind heart. You must learn to forgive others, especially those who hurt you. To be forgiven yourself, you must first forgive others. You need not be so prideful, also."

"What do you mean, prideful?" Jesse was not expecting that from Father.

With hands on Jess's shoulders, Father Diego explained that he didn't have to be the one to stand up to every wrong, and to let go of anger. Jesse pondered what the Father said. It wasn't making sense to him. Father then placed both hands on Jesse's head and recited Psalm 23. When it was over, Jesse hugged him hard.

"Jesse, remember this old Spanish proverb: No es suficiente que un hombre aprender a montar, tiene que aprender a caer. It is not enough for a man to learn how to ride: he must learn how to fall." With this said, they embraced again.

As he exited the church, Jesse wept like a child not for himself, but for those he left behind. Jesse was running from his past and from this present moment to begin the journey toward his future. He knew that in order for him to succeed, he must suffer, but not at the hands of the person who was supposed to love him. As he rode eastward, he hardened his heart not knowing what he would find. He was angry. He was looking for acceptance, he was looking for himself, and for most of all he was looking for love.

"Why can't someone love me? That's all I want. Why can't someone just love me for me?"

Even in his drunken state Carlos knew he said those words out of anger and didn't mean to say them out loud. Jesse left the church with Carlos watching him disappear into the night. He was riding in the direction of Mariposa; Carlos couldn't make himself say the words out loud. His prideful nature allowed Jesse to ride off. Carlos was proud of his son for standing up to him. He just didn't know how to say, I love you.

{Years earlier}
Everyone liked Jesse; he was an easy person to like. He always had a smile on his face, more often to hide the pain. He was very competitive when it came to play and work, but was always willing to lend a hand or an encouraging word to someone. He was always quick to give of himself, wanting nothing in return.

Jesse was a friend to everyone. He was raised to be a gentleman by his mother, aunts and the nuns. He was taught to rise when a lady entered or left a room and to answer 'Yes, ma'am and 'yes, sir'. He was to have decorum to open doors for ladies and to never raise his voice to elders. Jesse was raised in the Catholic ways. He attended 'Our Lady of Mercy.' He was dutiful student and learned his lessons well.

He was also a typical boy getting into mischief as all little boys do away from home and church. He never tolerated the bigger boys beating up on the little ones. He was primed to be set off with the least provocation when someone was mistreated. Jesse learned to fight early, and he was not going to lose many. He was raised to fight for what was right and to defend the weak.

Jesse was very quiet and reserved by nature. For his entire father's abuse, Jesse was a kind young man who looked for the good in everyone. He was also a young man with no experience with young ladies. This was difficult for him as he could not talk to his parents on this matter. So, he took all matters of the heart to the only person he could talk to, Padre Diego.

Because of his upbringing, he was not allowed to have company with young ladies until it was approved and arranged by his family. It was the custom of the family to have marriages arranged. Jesse wanted to love the person whom he was going to spend the rest of his life with. Jesse was growing up with thoughts of girls just like any young man's mind would be at his age. The restrictions placed on him and the way his father was with them only added to his resentment. He had to break away, and soon.

Sam was Jesse's best friend since he arrived into Merced. He knew how Jesse suffered, but Jesse still had this secrets and kept many thoughts to himself. He had many things to say, but for some reason, he could not even tell Sam, and he was his best friend.

He was always instructed by the nuns to confess to the priests. Jesse didn't see the need to. He always viewed the priests as just men. Jesse respected their authority; he just did not want to confess to or confide in another man except one. There was one man above all that Jesse respected, Padre Diego, and it was he that Jesse always came to when he was most troubled.

Lee Sheo was Jesse's friend also. Even though he was a few years younger, he was a friend who was closer than a brother and someone who Jesse would protect even if it would put his own life in danger. They met when the California Central Railroad was coming in from Sacramento down into San Joaquin Valley to unite the valley with Southern California.

Gin Sheo, Lee's father, was employed by the CCR to oversee the Chinese labor force. Ging was an educated man and spoke several languages. He was an engineer by education and a priest in his village in China. He fled China and ended up in England through his contacts at the university. There was a great civil war in China, and all priest were being imprisoned or killed.

Just after they arrived in Merced a series of robberies were reported. Because of the prejudice of the day the Chinese were easily given blame. The 'Don' was given authority to take care of these matters. An unidentifiable person in the crowd yelled out that the yellow boy Lee was the person.

"Besides, they all look alike, and what does it matter who takes the blame," The unidentified man yelled.

"Make an example of him regardless of age. The others will see what happens when they are caught!" Another voice shouted out. Typically, cowards find solidarity when they group up and place blame on those that are different.

Don Carlos had been drinking, and to make things worse, he was not in a good mood due to the railroad being out of schedule. He ordered the boy to be publicly whipped. Jesse was coming in from the fields and asked what was going on.

He was told who was going to be punished for the robberies. Jesse couldn't let this go on without saying something. He pleaded with his father, but his pleas fell on uncaring ears. Jesse quickly made up a lie that it was he who had stolen the articles. Jesse said this loud enough so the crowd would hear. The crowd drew quiet.

The 'Don' knew that he didn't do it. They were railroad tools and Jesse had no need for such things. What was the reason for this lie? Carlos just couldn't understand why Jesse would do this? Why would he put himself in middle of all this? Maybe it was another way to defy him. He knew that he couldn't say that Jesse was lying to protect this thief.

Carlos had to defend his name and save face not for the family but, for himself. A De La Souza would not tell a lie. He confessed that he stole and was ready to take his punishment. There were mixed emotions of Jesse confessing. They knew him and he couldn't have done it. As the town was growing in population, there were those who didn't know Jesse. They needed to see that the De La Souza were honorable, even though it meant the public whipping of his son.

Ging Sheo was on the job site miles away. He did not know that this was happening, and certainly would not have allowed this. The Chinese men were working, which left the women to witness this selfless act. To make this even more surprising was the fact that it was the Don's son who took the blame to help a Chinese boy.

The public whipping of a twelve-year-old was unheard of. The 'Don' was somewhat sadistically proud that Jesse took it like a man and did not even cry out very loud. Everyone spoke of the honor that the 'Don' had instilled in his family will still be intact. Juanita couldn't believe that Carlos would do such a thing. She arrived too late to stop it. She cried for Jesse and died a death that only a mother could for such cruelty. She also blamed Jesse for putting her through it.

Why does he do this to himself? She thought. She took him home. The next few days Jesse was kept inside and away from all. The event was soon forgotten and Jesse was allowed to help the Vaqueros bring in some cattle to the corrals. Jesse will forever have the marks on his back for the rest of his life. The physical scars will heal, knowing that he saved another will be with him forever.

Lee had been trying to find Jesse ever since that day. Lee was born in San Francisco and spoke English very well. He finally located Jesse at the DLS Corral next to the train station. Lee went over to thank Jesse and asked why he did what he did. They spent the day getting to know each other and they became as close as brothers.

After the day's chores were done, Lee and Jesse went into the woods to fish in the Cypress meadow ponds next to the grape vineyards. Ging Sheo was in the woods meditating when the boys came upon him. Jesse asked what he was doing. Lee said that his father was in meditation.

"What is meditation?" Jesse asked.

"This form of Zen mediation is controlling his mind so he can calm himself," answered Lee in a hushed voice.

"Are there other forms?" Jesse's curiosity was getting the best of him.

"Yes, there is a form that lets you endure physical pain," Lee said in even a softer voice.

"Let's not interrupt him," Lee put his finger over his mouth to show Jesse to stay quiet.

"Son, why do you disturb me when you know that this is my time to meditate? Ging said in a calm voice that was correcting, yet loving.

"Forgive me for my disturbance, father; I had no wish to dishonor you during your time of mediation," Lee answered with his head lowered to show respect.

"Who do we have here?" Ging Sheo asked his son.

"This is Jesse, the one I told you about," Lee answered.

"That was a noble act by taking punishment for something you did not do to help someone you did not know," Master Sheo said to Jesse without opening his eyes.

"But a lie is still a lie, the fact that you scarified yourself for someone else was honorable, "Master Sheo said with eyes still closed.

"Why would your Father allow this to happen?" Master Sheo finally opened his eyes.

"He knew I didn't do it. He wanted to save the family reputation, and I wanted to protect Lee."

"He dishonored himself, and you sacrificed yourself and brought honor to yourself."

"Lee tells me that you are a priest? A Catholic priest?" Jesse wanted to change the subject.

"No, not a Catholic priest, but a priest who meditates and who is in touch with the world around him," Master Sheo answered.

"I don't understand. You are different from the other priests in town," said Jesse.

"Would like to know more?" Master Sheo asked.

"Yes." Jesse wanted to know how this man could block out pain. Maybe it could work

with what he was going through. He
wanted to ease his pain, and mostly, he
wanted to forget.

The next day he started extra early in order
to finish his chores and assigned work so
he could meet Master Sheo in the grove of
Cypress along Bear Creek. Mariposa was
left to graze not too far from them.

"I brought along Sam to join us if you don't
mind, sir." Jesse wasn't sure if Sam could
join them.

"Do you have permission to be here?"
asked Master Sheo.

"Yes, sir," Sam answered with his head held
down.

"Pa works with the railroad and he knows
you. He said it was okay."

"And what does your mother say about it?"
The master asked.

"She thinks that you are the most polite
person she has ever met, and besides, I'm
with Jesse, too."

"Very well, let us begin," Master Sheo said.

He began with a statement, "The usefulness of a cup is its emptiness." Sam and Jesse looked puzzled by this statement. Jesse was being respectful by not interrupting, but he had a question on what the meaning of the statement was. He finally raised his hand as if he were in school.

Master Sheo recognized this gesture and acknowledged him. "It is not necessary to raise your hand; simply ask the question."

"I didn't want to interrupt you, sir," Jesse replied with Sam nodding his head in agreement.

"What if I had my eyes closed and did not see your hand? You would have left here without finding out what the statement meant."

"What does the statement mean, sir?" Jesse asked the question again.

"Ya, I had the same question," Sam added.

"The usefulness of a cup is its emptiness means, be prepared to accept new knowledge and not be hindered by old knowledge that has filled your head." The Master continued his lesson by giving examples of this thought.

"Seek knowledge; seek truth; just because you were told something doesn't make it true. When a father says things to their children, the truth of things could have been a prejudice handed down from generation to generation. I am not saying to not accept your parents' teaching but to look for the reason for things. Now, think of these things in silence." With the meaning given, it was now time for them to ponder things as Master Sheo intended.

For the next four years, Jesse learned various self-defense skills. Because of his strength of mind, he was allowed to learn various forms of meditation. Jesse was an enthusiastic pupil. Having Jesse there made it better for Lee, too. They each helped each other. Sam joined them whenever he could. All three were the best of friends.

"Remember that self-defense is just that; to defend one's self or someone who is in need of protection. Control your emotions and never take life unless it is necessary to protect yourself or others." Master Sheo was most adamant about this.

Even with all Master Sheo's teachings, Jesse was still missing something in his heart. He was missing the one. Because of these meditation methods, he became more aware of what he was being taught in the church. Visits to Father Diego became more regular, with questions becoming more direct. Jesse needed answers to his questions.

Jesse was becoming a man and now was more capable of defending the family and himself. His self-confidence grew with the passing years. His father raised him to not back down from a fight, for if he did, he would have to answer to him. He was gaining control of his emotions, but was he ready to confront his father?

Jesse was not like his brothers and sisters. He wanted more from life. The children had been raised without the gentle touch of a loving father. His mother tried her best. The children were growing up without the capability to express emotions. Jesse was different. He wanted it all, and he wanted all the good things life could give him. He wanted to feel wanted and loved.

The children were not to cry, but to take it. To show signs of weakness was not the De La Souza way. They were to be examples for others to see. Both Juanita and Carlos were raising children to be strong. The world was hard enough without having children cry for every little hurt. They were to pick themselves up and continue.

It was not the material things Jesse was after; it was what everyone needed. It was love. He had no idea what the word meant, let alone experience it. All he knew was that he needed more than what he was getting at home. Master Sheo, his aunts and uncles, and even the church showed more to him.

It was such a powerful emotion and the nuns always warned the young people of its dangers. Jesse had asked Sister Maria what it was like to be in love. She could not answer for she had never experienced it herself, other than the love for the church. Jesse wanted to know what love was and to have someone love him. What would it be like to have a girl?

{The encounter on the trail}
Jesse had time to think about what Father Diego said to him. He will miss the Father. Father Diego was more of a father than his own. He was patient, taught lessons about life, and was caring of one's thoughts and inner feelings. Foremost he was a teacher of the nature of God's creatures in the

environment.

As the night wore on, it occurred to him, how would he know what love was? He thought to himself that it will show itself one day and he would know. So not to worry about it, it will come in time.

For all the meditations he had learned from Master Sheo, it wasn't the controlling of his mind he was after, it was the presence of something greater than that. Jesse prayed for strength and courage to find his way. He was lost, and not from traveling in the dark. He was lost. He needed someone to help him find himself, someone to give him guidance, someone to show him the way. Jesse knew that he couldn't do this on his own.

Throughout his life, Jesse went to church and knew of God. It wasn't until he was in a crisis that he knew that he actually never asked God to enter his heart. He prayed out loud to God. He knew he was not worthy of this love, but he wanted it and needed it. He wept again, this time for himself. His heart was empty, and he wanted it filled. God answered at the moment when Jesse could not bear the thought of being alone any longer. He filled his heart. On this night, on top of his horse, he found the light he needed to guide him. With his heart heavy with shame, guilt, and the sin of his world, a miracle happened. He felt the weight of his soul lifted and cleansed. This time, he wept for joy; he wept for himself and for the first time forgave himself.

Jesse rode on through the night, knowing that he has the one he needed, the Lord. Someone loved him and all he had to do was to ask him in. Is it really that easy? It seemed to be. The burden of the night was lifted. How would it be for another person to accept him for himself, only asking in return to love unconditionally? Questions, questions without answers and no history of these feelings to draw from and the one who entered his heart this night did not answer them. In time his questions will be answered he decided. The emotional struggle was almost too much for him. He had to take control of his emotions. He prayed to his Savior, and then he meditated like Master Sheo taught him.

The night was long, but the road ahead was longer. Not knowing where to go, he rode on until Mariposa could not go any further. He stopped and made camp for the rest of the night and into the next day.

After caring for Mariposa and setting up camp, Jesse knelt and gave thanks to the one for watching over them. From that night forward, Jesse could not do anything without asking the Lord for guidance. Each morning and evening he would kneel and ask for forgiveness and give thanks. For the next several nights he dreamt of the events of the previous days and was still saddened for what had transpired. After several days at the same camp site, he knew it was time to quit thinking.

This morning he recited Psalm 23. The Lord is my shepherd; I shall not want. He maketh me lie down in green pastures; he leadeth me beside the still water. He restoreth my soul. After he prayed, he mounted Mariposa. It was time to go.

{Winter-lessons learned}

Now it was time to decide which trail to choose from. He decided to go east, following the trails to the Yosemite Valley and then across the Sierras to Nevada. He heard of a place called the Indian Territory east of New Mexico and thought that would be as good a place as any to call home for a while. He would then head to Missouri to visit his friend Sam in the spring.

Traveling this time of the year was an iffy

risk. You never knew when the weather would change on you. Winters in the high country were unforgiving, and all too often tragic. Jesse was neither outfitted for the journey nor trained; he was angry and hadn't thought it through.

He rode on to Mariposa, a small town just outside the Yosemite Valley. This was the same area where years earlier Mariposa, his horse, was captured. He stopped in the trading post to buy supplies, asked for directions, and spend a day or preparing for the journey.

The initial leg of his journey through the Sierras into Nevada, Jesse found hazardous. The winter's storms were unpredictable this time of the year. If he would have injured himself or Mariposa he would have not survived the high country. He was sure of himself, but the truth was, he was ill-prepared for this type of journey. Even for a boy with all the confidence in the world he would not have known how to survive. Even with the best survival training, it would have been perilous. The nights were so agonizing bitter. He was scared and had second thoughts for leaving home.

In the morning, he decided to push on.

Jesse was upset with himself for having second thoughts. He wasn't one to give in to his fears. He was acting as a child would. He had to deal with them. He meditated until the feeling left him.

The second night he came across a one-room cabin big enough for him and Mariposa to share. It looked like it not had been used for some time. Nonetheless, it was shelter enough for this night. He gathered what tender he could find and lit the wet wood. It smoked for a while, then it took fire.

A roof overhead, a warm fire, and a hot meal of salted pork with a pot of coffee guaranteed he would sleep tonight. Mariposa had some oats that Jesse bought from the trading post. The wind picked up. He could hear ice peppering the windows. If the weather held, he would be on the windward side of the mountain by midafternoon. With any luck, he would make it to Aurora by sundown.

It snowed heavily during the night. The wind was blowing ice pellets, and he had to decide to either go on or stay another day. With the likelihood of being snowed in, he decided to make the ridge and down to Aurora. It was a gamble he had to take.

The sky was threatening, a gloomy sky that covered the sun. With the wind coming down the face of the mountain, the ice pellets were piercing his face. Jesse packed quickly wasted little time and departed. His decision to leave was a life and death decision for the both of them.

At times he had to dismount to walk some distance because the snow was too deep for Mariposa to carry him. By almost sundown, he saw the faint lights of a town. Relieved that they were almost there, he urged Mariposa to pick up the pace to get them off the mountain and into town before nightfall came. A snow storm was about to cover the area.

Jesse found himself in Aurora, Nevada, where the early winter storms ended all travel in or out until the late spring. Aurora was a mining town located in Mineral County, near the towns of Bodie and Hawthorne. Gold was discovered in the late 1850's. The town was governed by both California and Nevada until it was determined that the town was indeed within the Nevada state boundary by three miles.

Jesse secured a job working in one of the

saloons sweeping, cleaning, and doing whatever was needed during business hours. Being a boom mining town, the saloons were open day and night. At least he was inside out of the cold and had a roof over his head. He had a room upstairs. It was loud, but it was warm and dry. Mariposa had a stable stall and out of the weather.

There was no mail in or out until late spring. No word of his whereabouts could be sent home. Those who cared about him would spend a winter wondering if he was out of harm's way. He didn't want anyone to worry, but he could do nothing about it until spring.

 The work was easy enough, if it weren't for the ill-mannered and those who weren't properly house-broken. Men who congregated in mining towns were vulgar, foul mouthed, and had the hygiene of a horse. For the most part, the "working" women of the brothels were not much better.

The saloon girls were different. They were there for conversation and to entice men to buy more drinks. These women were not there to sell their bodies. These women were young and easy on the eye, and most well no more than 16-18 years old.

Men came to town to buy supplies, drink, and to have a good time. Some came to find other things. Some men came to prey on other men. When men, women and drink come together, trouble was not far behind. This town was no different from any other disorderly mining town of its day.

There was a sheriff in town, but he was usually prospecting his own claim. Most lawmen didn't know much about the law. They were gunmen of bad reputation hired by store owners to keep stealing down and keep some sort of order at any cost.

The sheriff's two deputies were the ones who kept order. Some men enjoy giving pain to others for no other reason than it gives them enjoyment. These deputies took liberties on the weak. The badges on their chests gave license to intimidate.

Most boom towns didn't have much law or order. It seemed that the only law was kept by either with fists or guns. The real laws were concerned with rustling of cattle and horses. These seemed to rile men the most. Most arguments were taken care of with the guy. As long as it was a fair fight, the local law didn't interfere.

Jesse did his work without complaint. He saw men so drunk they would pass out on the spot. He would have to help carry them to a chair and leave them there. He saw men shot for just the sake of argument. Many men were killed for just cheating at cards. The saloons were filled with cigarette smoke, spilled drinks, tobacco spit, cheap perfume and the stench of men who hadn't bathed. Every night, Jesse had to mop the floors where alcohol vomit was. The livery stable smelled better. At winter's end, miners were at their nastiest. The cold and the snows prevented them from digging. Monotony always brought out the worst in everyone. With nothing to do, men's tempers were at their quickest.

One evening in late March, Old John, a worn out soul of about 60 years old reached both his limits. Jesse learned to watch his surroundings while working in the saloon. He never knew when a fight would break out. It was a daily occurrence. The old-timer was usually obnoxious for a bit, and then he would find a place to pass out. He was regular, and Jesse knew he meant no harm, and so did everyone else.

This night one of the deputies had too much to drink and decided that he would hassle the miner. It was obvious that the drunken miner was meaning no harm and was heading out, calling it a night. The deputy went to see if he could coerce him into a fight.

With the miner drunk, it wasn't difficult to force him to react. Old John pulled his revolver out, but being so intoxicated, he couldn't hit a thing. The deputy shot Old John in the chest. He was taken to the Doc's and there he stayed until morning when he was pronounced dead. Because of the weather, extra graves were usually dug in the late fall. The winter months didn't allow the digging of them because the ground was frozen. They were covered over with wooden planks until needed. The graves used during winter were covered with snow until the ground thawed. Then the bodies were covered with soil. Most of them were unmarked, as miners tended not to have family to visit them.

Because the local law intimidated the miners, the deputy was acquitted of the shooting by jurors of miners. The sheriff and the other deputy testified that the miner provoked the fight and drew his gun, even though they had their backs to the confrontation in question. Jesse knew that the jury of miners didn't want this happening to them. Since Old John had no next of kin, the judge claimed the rights to the mine. The miners were ready to riot. They needed someone to lead them but until that happened, they would have to take it.

It wasn't but a few days later that everyone put the incident behind them. For Jesse, it stuck in his gut. He knew this type of injustice could happen to anyone at any time. It was wrong. The judge, sheriff and deputies were corrupt.

It hadn't been a week when the same deputy singled out the youngest saloon girl and harassed her into going upstairs with him. She clearly did not want his hands on her. Howard, the owner of the saloon, tried to redirect the deputy's attention. What he got was a pistol butt to his head.

Elizabeth was her name, she was not older than 17. Jesse liked her right off. She was new to this type of work. She came from San Francisco and was working her way eastward. She had a cousin in Chicago, Illinois, where she was trying to get to. She had no other family.

She was saving her money to take a stage and then a train to her cousin. She didn't like the work, but for a single girl, it was all there was. She had straw colored hair, eyes of blue, and stood about five foot. Jesse called her 'Little Bit', He fancied her. He had no real interest in her but for a friend. He watched her to make sure she was treated well by the men. On their breaks, they would go upstairs to eat their meals to get away from the stench of the saloon. They were close in age, so they got along well.

They kept each other company. They shared a common door between them. When it came to private thoughts, they didn't go there. They both kept that from each other. On their time off, they spent it together. The bond was that of a brother and sister. Jesse made sure that she got in okay, checking on her and just being there for her when she became ill. He felt at home watching over her, just like he had done with his family. He was protective of her, and it was in his nature to be so.

Jesse went over to help Howard. He was met with a pistol poking him in the chest. Jesse was unarmed. The room went still to see what would happen next. Jesse knew he was not in a position to do much with a gun in his chest. He backed away, controlling his emotions.

The deputy continued his advancement on the girl. Howard's persistent interfering earned him a second gun butt across his right eye. This time it opened a cut above his eye that required stitching. Blood covered Howard's face. This was getting out of hand. The sheriff and the other deputy continued to have their dinner without concerning themselves.

Jesse couldn't let this go. He went upstairs and strapped on his Remingtons. He had never pointed a gun at another man. He just knew he had to do something to protect Little Bit. It was apparent that no other man was going to come to her aid. The only decent man was pistol whipped for helping. By the time he came back down the other girls were trying to separate Little Bit from the deputy. This was just too much for Jesse to bear.

Continuing downstairs, he looked to where the other two were. They had their backs to the whole thing, obviously enjoying the control they had on the town. As soon as he reached the bottom of the stairs, he yelled out to the deputy to take his hands off of her. It looked as if she had been slapped around some. Blood was coming out of her nose and her dress was torn, exposing her naked back. She was covering herself as best she could. Jesse was beyond anger. He was prepared to do damage. The deputy shoved her down. The other girls took her and covered her. He made his way to Jesse. The other two were now up out of their chairs facing the scene, guns still lashed down. They had nothing to fear from this boy. Assessing the situation, Jesse wanted this to end peacefully if possible. If not, he would do whatever it took to end it. Taking deep breaths he controlled himself and didn't panic.

"This doesn't concern you, boy," The deputy said, slurring his words.

"I'm afraid it does now. Leave her alone," said Jesse. He didn't want to fight. He didn't have any experience doing this. He had to keep his composure and remember what he had learned. He had to control his breathing and to be aware of his surroundings. This wasn't a neighborhood bully; this was a man who could kill him.

"Why don't we just let this go?" Jesse wanted to avoid having to shoot someone or be shot.

"It's too late for that," The deputy had his gun aimed at Jesse.

"Everyone here heard that I wanted to end this peacefully, so whatever happens from this point will be on his account. All of you are witnesses to this. Okay, deputy, it's your call," Jesse shouted it out so everyone could hear.

"I am going to teach you some respect, boy. I've see how you are always looking at her," The deputy took off his gun belt and motioned Jesse to do the same.

"I am going to beat you first and then take the girl and make you watch." The deputy rolling up his shirt sleeve in anticipation of the fist fight.

"You are a deputy, and I don't want to fight you. If you want to fight, you'll have to take off your badge." When the deputy takes his badge off he will became just a common citizen. Jesse wanted to make some time so he could think about all his options. He was hoping the miners would step in and help out. It was not to come. They were all afraid.

Jesse took his gun belt off, but before he handed it to the owner of the saloon, he unlashed and cocked both revolvers in case he needed them. He knew that he had to defend himself using what he learned from Master Sheo. This was for real now. He had to relax and concentrate.

"Boy, you should have left this alone," The deputy took another shot of whiskey as the other two law men sat back down.

The deputy made an attempt to hit Jesse. Jesse stepped to the side and the deputy missed, exposing his throat. Jesse's open right hand caught the exposed throat with such force that he crushed the deputy's larynx. The deputy fell to his knees and then went face down, grabbing his throat and gasping for air. The sounds of whizzing air and gurgling blood were the only sounds made.

Howard quickly tossed Jesse's guns to him. Jesse had them out before the sheriff and deputy had theirs out. It happened so fast that the lawmen didn't have time to unleash them from their holsters. Jesse didn't have time to think about anything else but to shoot them.

"Hold on there; we have to take you in for

killing him," The sheriff called out with both having their hands on their guns.

"The code of the West says that I had every right to defend myself. Your deputy was in the wrong. We have witnesses to that effect. He came after me. He took his badge off." Jesse had both revolvers aimed, one at the sheriff and the other at the deputy.

The West had a code that said people did not have a duty to retreat when threatened. The Indiana Supreme Court upheld the 'no duty to retreat' code. Since the deputy removed his badge, he was not acting in an official capacity. He was an ordinary citizen at that point. Jesse had every right to defend himself.

The room became alive with the shouting of the miners agreeing. They had someone they could follow even if it was a boy of sixteen. Jesse was the first to stand up for them. The sheriff took notice of the situation, knowing that the crowd was on the side of the saloon boy. Both he and the deputy withdrew their hands from their side arms, and then walked backwards out of the saloon. Moments later, the deputy came in with his pistol out. Without thinking, Jesse shot him in the gun hand wrist twice. Even though he was left handed he was ambidextrous and fired one shot from each of the Remington. The caliber of his Remington all but severed the deputy's hand.

"I'm coming in! Don't shoot!" The sheriff came in with both hands held up so everyone could see. He came to retrieve the deputy. Jesse walked over to the sheriff with both guns cocked. He stopped inches away from him.   He raised both guns to the sheriff's forehead. The sheriff, feeling the heat from the guns, closed his eyes. Jesse was incensed at this point. He could have killed the both of them. Little Bit yelled Jesse's name. He had to regain control of himself. He didn't want to become them. What he did was brand the sheriff and deputy with the ends of his Remingtons on their foreheads and then took the guns and holsters from both men.

"I will remember you. These markings will ensure that," With that said, he let them go.

"It's over, you okay?" Jesse went over to Little Bit to console her. With all the excitement over, the miners went to Jesse offering congratulations with extended hands and pats on the back. Offers of free drinks came from many. Jesse wanted none of this, all he wanted was to take Little Bit away from all this.

"No, yes, I don't know," she said, with tears running down her face. He helped her upstairs to her room. He waited outside her door until she changed into her nightgown. His guns were unlashed just in case they come back to attempted to arrest him. She invited him in. He spent the night holding her. Knowing the type of men they were, he knew that he had to be on his guard. It was late March, and the snows would soon be gone.

He couldn't sleep; he had taken a man's life and shot another. He was visibly shaken. He would have to deal with this later. Right now, she needed him more. How can people be so cruel? He had to calm himself. He must not let this change him. He was not a cruel person and didn't want to be. He wanted to be everything his father wasn't. He confessed to the one, knowing that he was now in jeopardy of going to hell for his actions. He did what he thought was right; protect life and defend those who could not defend themselves.

For the rest of the winter, the sheriff and

deputy were on their guard. Since that night, the miners didn't allow themselves be bullied anymore. They stood their ground and backed each other. Bullies are bullies when they know that they have you afraid. In time, both men left town, fearful for their lives. The judge also left. Rumor has it that the sheriff was killed in nearby Bodie. The whereabouts of the judge and the other deputy were not known.

With the winter almost over, the roads were beginning to clear. It was time for Little Bit and Jesse to leave town and continue on their journeys. Little Bit was insufficient in money, so Jesse gave her what she needed and then some for the trip east to her cousin. She was taking the stage until she got to a large enough town where she would take the train to Chicago. He wanted her to be able to go home. He was homeless and knew what that felt like.

"I don't know what to say," Little Bit was overwhelmed by the kindness Jesse showed.

Take it, I have plenty," Jesse said holding her hand.

"How can I ever repay you for this?" Tears were forming at the corners of his eyes.

"Someday when I'm in Chicago, I'll look you up and you can buy me dinner or something," Little Bit hugged him and kissed his cheek.

"For now, I'll follow you to the next rest station," Jesse reassuring her that he will be with her along the way.

"Good. Why don't you come all the way to Chicago?" Elizabeth liked Jesse. She now had feelings for him. She had more than a sibling love, she was falling in love with him.

"That sounds inviting, but I have someone to go see," Jesse was still rubbing her hands with both of his.

People do things to get by; sometimes it goes against what they know to be right. Little Bit had no choice. She found herself in bad circumstances. Luckily, she found a friend in Jesse. Jesse had someone, too, all he had to do was open his heart and talk to him.

Mariposa was kept in the livery stable most of the winter, which she didn't like. The saloon and livery stable were owned by the same person. Howard witnessed what he did for Elizabeth. Before Jesse left, Howard gave him a bag of feed for Mariposa.

He followed the stage coach until they came to the first rest station. He stayed the night there. When it was time for supper, he feed Mariposa first, and inside the bag of grain he discovered an envelope. It was full of money and a note thanking him for what he did that night in protecting Elizabeth and him.

You give, and it is given back to you. Jess didn't expect this gift. The bag of grain was enough. The next morning he was up early. It was going to be a long ride. The more he thought about it, the more it made sense to catch a train to Dodge City, Kansas, and then head down to the Indian Territory. He had enough money to do so now. The stage was ready to leave. The stage had a new team. Passengers were fed and rested. With the stage ready, Little Bit and Jesse said their goodbyes.

"Good-bye, Little Bit, I mean Elizabeth. Take care," Jesse and Little Bit hugged once more.

"I like you calling me Little Bit. It makes me feel like you are my boyfriend and we had given each other nicknames that only we knew of. Goodbye Jesse, thank you for everything. I won't forget you," They hugged until she started to cry. They held each other not like before. They both looked up, and something stirred in their hearts. She kissed him fully on the mouth. It was a kiss filled with passion and he kissed her back. It excited him. She boarded the stage holding onto his hand, and tried to urge him inside. He wanted to, but he had to follow his heart.

As the stage departed, Little Bit opened the stage doors, waving good bye and pleading for him to change his mind and come to Chicago. He waved back and yelled that someday he would meet up with her again. He turned around and wiped his eyes when no one was watching, acting as though dust had blown into his eyes.

She will be missed. He knew that he had feelings for her. He didn't know how to tell her. Maybe it was best this way. He was on a quest. He had unanswered questions. He had to find answers and to prove to himself that he was a man. Anger and youthful pride drove him on. Jesse readjusted his gear and mounted Mariposa. He was heading to the next train station. There was no urgency. He was enjoying being outside and riding once again. It was an experience being in Aurora. Hopefully, the next town he finds will be more settled.

They traveled some distance before they reached a town. Jesse was tired, and Mariposa needed new shoes. It was perfect timing that he came into town when he did. He caught the furrier in time. A hot bath, a good steak, and a good night's rest were all what was on Jesse's mind. Not being on a horse for the entire winter, Jesse was not in riding form. Even Mariposa was winded easily. They were both out of practice. The both needed a good night's rest.

After dinner, Jesse wandered around town to see what he could see. Like in most towns, the local saloon was where the most action was found. He wasn't looking for that type of action. He spent the winter having all the action he ever wanted to see. He had enough of this day. All he wanted was to go to bed. He making his way to the hotel when he was stopped by a figure coming out of the alley.

"Hey boy, you didn't finish what you started," A voice from the dark said.

"What?" Jesse was straining to see who it

was.

"You thought that you were just going to ride out of town without paying for what you did?" A familiar sound of a gun being drawn from a holster with the all too familiar sound of a revolver being cocked was heard.

"Who are you?" Jesse pulling his coat aside to expose his Remingtons. Jesse widened his stance and lowered his hips to ready himself. The figure stepped into the gas lamp lit walkway in front of the hotel. It was the former deputy that left Aurora.

"You thought you were done with it," The deputy slid his overcoat over his hip, exposing his intentions. His was healed on his left side, gun unlashed and cocked.

"I'm done with it!" Jesse wanted no part of this.

"I'm not done with it. I wanted you to know who it was before I killed you." The former deputy stepped toward Jesse. Jesse had no choice but to pull his revolver faster than the deputy thought anyone could.

"What's this?" The town sheriff came up

from behind Jesse.

The deputy drew his gun and shot the sheriff by mistake. Jesse shot the former deputy in the chest and the forehead. He was killed instantly. The sheriff was shot in the shoulder. Jesse carried the sheriff to the hotel and stayed with him until the town doctor came.

"What was that about?" The sheriff asked.

"Some unfinished business from Aurora this winter that I thought was finished," Jesse was calming himself.

"You okay?" the sheriff asked Jesse.

"I should be asking you," Jesse replied.

{Letter home}

Father Juan Diego
Our Lady of Mercy
San Joaquin Valley
Merced, California

March 30, 1890
Dear Padre Diego,

All is well with me; I spent the winter in Aurora, Nevada. I found work sweeping and cleaning. Not what I was raised to do, but it was a job, and it kept Mariposa and I

sheltered with our bellies filled.

I hope this letter finds you all well. Because I don't know what my father would do with this letter, I am writing to you so you can tell my family that I am fine and that I left Aurora as soon as the weather permitted. I am fixing to head to the Indian Territory, Oklahoma. With good fortune and good weather, I will find myself there by summer's end.

My final destination is Mansfield Missouri. That is where Sam and his family's farm are. I plan to stay with them until I can return as a man with something to offer.

Inform Sister Maria that I will stay true to myself and keep in mind the lessons she taught. As for the teachings you taught, how can I thank you? I have taken the time to gaze at God's work along the way. How perfect is his work, how intricately woven are we together, each thing serving a purpose. Thank you for being there for me. Oh, by the way, I have found him along the way. You were right, what a blessing knowing that you are never alone. He has strengthened me as I traveled to unknown places. I read daily from the book and find that there are many lessons yet to learn in my life.

Tell my mother the reasons why I had to do this. I plan to come back when I have found what I was looking for. Every now and again, I will send a letter to let you all know where I am. Because I will be traveling, you can not correspond. When I settle for the winter, I will send you an address where you can write.

I plan to take a train to Dodge City, Kansas, where I will work for a bit, then head to the Indian Territory. I am sending my love to all.

Con Dios, Jesse

{A horse is a horse unless it's your horse}
Mariposa was a temperate horse which took to Jesse's every command. Each one seemed to know the other's thoughts. It was more than a friendship that bound them together. It was as if they were psychologically linked. Mariposa anticipated his every wish without words spoken.

Mariposa got her name from the mining town near the Valley of Yosemite where she was captured. The name given to her by Jesse comes from the Spanish word, which means butterfly. This name fits her; she has a calm demeanor and poised on her feet. She has a placid spirit. She is a mustang, a Spanish horse that is as resilient as the country. She was a mustang but possessed traits that were from the Andalusian breed. Jesse had never seen a mare so black in color with beautiful eyes. She stood 15 hands tall; tall for a mare. She was physically very muscular, more so than the average mustang mare. She has a compact build, long thick mane and tail with a massive chest.

As the Conquistadores left this country and went back to Spain, they left some horses behind due to thefts by Native Americans. Through the generations, the Mustangs roamed free. They evolved into a breed that fit the frontier. They are intelligent and have a fighting spirits. A Mustang's awareness to risk will not let them get into dangerous situations.

As a child, Mariposa and Jesse were inseparable, with Jesse even spending his nights in her stall asleep. Her eyes were not the eyes of a horse. She possessed the eyes of a spirit,"Espiritu Ojos de Caballos" the Vaqueros would say. Jesse found her to be responsive and obedient. The Vaqueros watched them together and knew that Jesse possessed the "spirit" of the horse. Mariposa was not tethered at night and was found wherever Jesse was.

{Oklahoma-Red Earth}
The journey east from Aurora went without much difficulty or incident. It had been two years since that night, many towns were traveled through, and many friends were made with stories to tell his children someday. He stayed in Dodge City longer than he intended, a year longer.

Oklahoma, "the land of the red man," came from the Choctaw language. This was where his trail was to end for the summer and then to Missouri in the spring. They both were tired. Having traveled along way, it was time for them to settle down and rest.

He had let all those who cared for him know how his travels were going. He apologized to Sam for taking so long to reach him. He would mail the letters in the first town he came to. He had one more winter stay, and then he would be in Missouri.

The ride into the territory was a long dry one. There was a lot of activity by the Calvary. They were on patrol to secure the area from outlaws and troublesome renegades in the territories. Jess was stopped on occasion to be questioned.

Mariposa and Jesse had just about enough of the dust and sun. They stopped at the edge of the river, found a crossing and crossed over. Once across, he dismounted and took a drink and filled his canteen.

"They call this river the Cimarron, I think, or maybe it's the Canadian?" Jesse said to Mariposa as she was gulping down large quantities of water.

"Sure is muddy for a river. Careful not to drink too much now, it tastes like it has some salt in it. It sure doesn't look like much this part of the country. Where are the trees? I guess it beats being in Kansas. Looks nothing like California. Nothing looks like California, that's a fact, maybe

The High Colorado," Mariposa shook her head as if she agreed with Jesse.

"I miss the clear cool clean waters of the Sierras coming into the San Joaquin," Jesse wetting his handkerchief and wiping the back of his neck.

"We'll stop and stay for a while the next town we get to. We'll over winter there. It's getting to be late July or early August maybe? No time to be traveling any further this year. I hear that this part of the country gets funny weather," Jesse talking to Mariposa as if she understood him.

Jesse made camp for the night. Mariposa's rig was taken off. She was left to graze as he went to hunt up dinner. With the weather being so warm, he took off his chinks. They protected him from brush, but now that he was making camp, he didn't want to sweat so much.

He was gone for maybe 10 minutes when he heard Mariposa as if she was in distress. Thinking that it was some large animal stalking her, he made his way to the camp as quickly as his legs could carry him. Running through shrubs that bore spines, they pierced his leggings. He took no heed to them. His friend was in trouble.

He found an Indian party looting his camp. Each one had painted faces of red. One was looking in his saddle bags while the other two were trying to take hold of Mariposa's lead. The most noticeable feature was their scalp locks, which were made to stand erect with red paint. The hair was made to resemble a horn. It was a strange sight; nonetheless, they were fierce-looking men.

Jesse had his rifle trained on the one looting his saddle bags. He fired a warning shot into the air to get their attention. They all stopped and looked in the direction of Jesse. Every one of them, including Jesse, froze at this point. Jesse had no intention of shooting any of them unless they gave cause to. He was remembering Ging Sheo's words. Self-defense is to defend, not to take life.

The three slowly backed away from the camp. They were armed with bows and arrows along with knives. They made no attempt to charge Jesse. Accessing the situation, they figured that even with the three of them, it would have been foolish to attack someone with a repeating rife already aimed at them. Jesse would have shot them without hesitation if he thought they were going to hurt Mariposa.

With a whistle, Mariposa came to Jesse's side. The three painted men looked at other and were amazed that such an animal would come on command. They lowered their weapons and extended their hands to show that they wanted to de-escalate the situation. Jesse did the same with his rifle but unlashed his side arms just in case they changed their stance. He was cautious and didn't want to give them the impression that he was an easy mark he wanted to end this with everyone breathing, including himself.

All four struck a peaceful coexistence for the moment. Jesse did not understand their language but did understand that they wanted to make peace. What Jesse did not understand was that it was their way to steal horses. It brought honor to them. Each tribe had its measure of what brings honor to its men.

Because of his actions, he was measured as a great warrior. They did not believe him to be weak. It took more courage to capture an enemy and then let his enemy go free. Since Jesse was not a member of an enemy tribe, this peace accord was the honorable thing to do. As men do at a peace camp, they exchanged gifts. The leader of the band gave Jesse a knife. Jesse in return gave him one of his bowie knives. It was an even trade, but more than that, it sealed the friendship amongst them.

"What are your names, and which tribe are you from?" Asked Jesse. They looked at each other, trying to understand his question.

"Pointing to himself, he said, "Jesse," The leader pointed in kind and said "Chaticks-si-Chaticks" which meant Men of Men.

It was Jesse's turn to try to comprehend. He repeated his name pointing to himself. "Jesse De La Souza."

The leader of the band again pointed to himself and his companions. "Chaticks-si-Chaticks, Pariki."

Moments later, he said in barely audible English, "Pawnee."

"I get it," Jesse finally understood. They were the Pawnee tribe.

It would have turned out tragically if Jesse reacted differently when he found them with Mariposa. In retrospect, it was much better this way. He didn't want to make enemies. They said their good-byes and with that, Jesse felt like he accomplished something. In a strange land, it was good to have all the friends you can find. He looked his new knife and was impressed with the skill of the workmanship.

He had been impressed with all the tribes he had encountered. He tried to learn something from each one. Each had its own way of surviving the land in which its members chose to live. They took what the land offered founding food, sheltering materials, clothing materials and medicines.

They retrieved their horses from the thicket. Jesse was taken by the ease in which each mounted his horse. He was remembering how the Plains Indians would do the same with the effortless motion without the aid of stirrups or a saddle horn. They were truly horsemen.

They all had one thing in common the love of family and friends. They would defend them to the death. Yes, each tribe had its enemies, but so do the white men, or any man. Each tribe took only what nature gave and no more. They did not devastate the land for profit; they lived in harmony with it. Jesse couldn't say that about the so-called civilized men.

The Native American practiced their religions which were handed down through the generations as far back as the old ones could remember. They were here before the white men came into the land. Their ways were practiced for thousands of years.

Since the first landing of Europeans, Native Americans had been dying by the thousands due to introduced diseases in which they had no inherited immunity. The Pilgrims survived the first years in the Americans due to the indigenous tribes in the area helping them. They themselves were weakened by disease brought over. With their help, the first Americans survived.

Later the white man came and told them they were savages. Was it not the reason for the whites coming to the Americans to have religious freedom? Throughout the ages, religion was used as the reason to civilize Native Americans. Many lives were lost in the quest for this. Cultures were lost in the pursuit of making them civilized; many scarifies were made in this religious mission on both sides.

White men say that thy discovered this land, but the fact remains that the Native Americans were here before recorded time. No one discovered this land. It was here before they arrived and will be here after everyone is gone.

And so a country was founded on the principle.....**That all men are created equal and that they are endowed by their Creator with certain unalienable rights, among these the right to life, liberty, and pursuit of happiness....** how ironic these words were written by men who themselves were persecuted for wanting to be free men, and yet could not stand free men who were different from themselves.

Along his travels Jesse had been fortunate to have made friends with the Native Americans. They certainly have been shown that the white man was one not to be trusted. They have destroyed their way of life and murdered them for the sake of gaining more land and the riches from the land.

Jesse found the Native Americans to be generous, hospitable, and wanting to live in peace with the white man. Our ways seem just as strange to them as theirs are to us. Of course there are exceptions, as there are exceptions to the white leaders who truly want to have peace with them.

As the day passed into night, Jesse dozed in a half sleep. A dream woke him. He was still hurting over the incident with his father, but even more depressed for having to leave his brothers and sisters behind to face it. He couldn't sleep, so he saddled Mariposa and broke camp before first light.

"Okay, the first appearance of a town we come to we will over winter, then head to Missouri," Mariposa whinnied as if she understood.

The Indian Territory was being settled at this time; small towns were springing up along the rail lines. The railroads were given land in exchange for bringing in the lines to connect the west to the east and the north to the south. Tent cities give rise to towns along the rail lines. Concessions were made to the railroads. The federal government paid for the lines to lay the rail at a cost of $16,000 per mile on the flat lands and $48,000 on mountainous terrain. Immigrants from China, Ireland, and Mexico all came to work on the rail lines.

The railroads could also buy tracts of land 10 square miles on either side of the track. Later, the area that the railroad received was 20 miles on either side. The safeguard against a monopoly of land, railroads could only purchase the land in a checkerboard pattern. As time passed, the railroad paid settlers to buy the adjacent parcels of land, but the RR kept the deeds. With all the railroads coming in all over the country, towns sprang up along the rail line water stations. The Valley of the Still Waters was such a town. The territorial land run of 1889 brought civilization to the Indian Nations frontier.

Captain David Payne left the military and tried to settle the area in the 1880's. His group were known as "Boomers." The groups were mostly Kansans who were looking for free land. Captain Payne made several attempts to settle the area, only to die in Kansas before his dream could be fulfilled. David Couch would take over the group, and later, his group was successful in establishing a settlement in the Still Water creek area.

Jesse arrived two days later in a small settlement. The Cavalry was stationed in the area. They arrived at the livery stable right before the noon stage came rolling in. Both were in need of something to eat and rest.

"What is the name of this place?" Jesse asked the livery attendant.

"Some folks around here call this place the Valley of the Still Waters," answered the attendant.

"Long name for a small place," Jesse said.

"They named the town for the creek that flows through here. It seems that it is always full of water, but it doesn't move very fast. Most who call this place home call it Still Waters." Jesse paused for a moment thinking that this town was his destiny. Father Diego's voice echoed in his head. He leadeth me to still waters.

An elderly gentleman was coming upon them and overheard their conversation. He added his version (which is the true reason for the name). He seemed to be a learned man by the way he spoke and dressed. Perhaps he was the town's mayor or something to that effect.

"That is part true; Henry Ellsworth (Indian commissioner) around 1832 set out on an expedition to survey and describes the new land. He brought along a noted writer by the name of Washington Irving, and he described the area. He named the area The Valley of the Still Waters, and the name was shortened to Still Waters."

"How do you know this?" Jesse asked.

"I am the school master, and it's my job to know why," And with that, he walked away rather smugly. Both the livery man and Jesse shrugged their shoulders and went on about their business.

{Vaquero style}
Jesse began loosening the chest strap and removed the California Saddle. The saddle and tack were the finest that money could buy. The rig was edged in silver and made from the finest leather. The saddle was ornately tooled with silver, and the leather was engraved with design.

The skirt was squared with extra wide fenders. Carols De La Souza may not have been a good father, but he made sure that the children had what was needed to make a good impression of being a De La Souza. He had bought all the finery that a 'Vaquero' would ever need. What he couldn't buy was respect from Jesse.

Chinks were the style of the modern Vaquero's outfit instead of chaps. Chinks are a half-length chap that attaches at the waist and ends just below the knee, usually with a very long fringe at the bottom and along the sides which makes them appear much longer than they were. This was to keep the horses' sweat from the riders' legs and to protect them from brush.

The outfit is a cross between a batwing (full-length chap wrapped around and held up by a belt) and a shotgun (chaps worn like pants); each leg usually has two fasteners located high up on the thigh. These were cooler to wear than a full chap, which is why they were adopted for usage by southwestern cowboys.

Jesse's boots were fitted with border tooled spur straps with spots and Conchos with family initials, DLS. The spurs were made of silver. On his belt was a San Francisco Bowie knife with sheath.

Cuffs had two functions. One was to protect store bought shirts, which were very expensive. The second function was to protect wrists from kicking hooves from the cattle. Both the chinks and the cuffs had the De La Souza brand.

Most Vaqueros carried a lemon along with suet with them to rub on the la riata's (restas) to keep them from becoming too stiff. Most are made from bull hide with a length of 80 feet. Jesse's lay was a stiff one for heel roping.

Jesse's hat was the traditional Spanish Gaucho (4 inch round rim), black in color. Jesse had just bought a new Winchester Deluxe with a Lyman rear sight and a Beech's combination front sight.

His uncles gave him for his birthday two Remington .44-40 caliber revolvers with 5 3/4" silver barrels with his family name engraved on the barrels instead of the handles. His two gun rig was a rooter closed toe. Jesse was predominately left handed but used his right hand almost equally. Most boys were changed over to use their right arm only; Jesse was allowed to use both. He was the only left-handed boy in the whole De La Souza family. He was especially proud of the revolvers, for it meant that he was no longer considered a child. He was very close to his uncles. They treated him well.

A man usually received his first side arm from his father, but in this case his great uncles, Tio Alonzo, and Tio Edmundo, had the honor of doing so. Jesse wore the finest riding clothing that money could buy. He would have traded all of it for just having the love of his father and his family near. Why does life have to be so complicated? All he wanted was to be wanted.

{First Impression}

The passengers were being let off this time. He was facing the sun and could not see their faces. He was not paying much attention to them until the stage had actually left the station and gone on to the watering pond. There was only one main pond within the area. This pond was used by everyone, from watering horses to the volunteer firefighters in case of fire. A school house was being constructed not too far from it. The Oklahoma Agricultural and Mechanical College was temporarily being housed in a church until the construction of the college was completed within a couple of years.

The town was a charming, quaint little town. There was a livery stable, feed store, small hotel where the stage was located, general store, a rail station at the edge of town and a restaurant. There was even a Cavalry outpost on the out skirts of town. A sign giving directions to a government subsidized ranch for the army horses and beef was posted on the Cavalry post. Forts in the area at this time were Fort Sill (near present day Lawton), Fort Reno (4miles west of present day El Reno), Fort Gibson and Fort Smith, Arkansas. After the inaugural land run of 1889, tent cities along the railways sprang up. These tent cities such as Oklahoma City, Kingfisher, El Reno, Norman, Guthrie and Stillwater, grew from near zero populations at day break to thousands by night fall.

Jesse wanted to someday attend a university to study business and botany. He wanted to own a vineyard one day. The Northern California area was perfect for such a venture. Jesse remembered the countryside between Madrid and Santander where the vineyards stretched out as far as the eye could see. The region near Burgess is known for Merlot and Cabernet Sauvignon grapes.

Jesse had spent many fall days working in the vineyard cutting the vines so the next area could be planted with grafted new varieties. In the early to mid-spring, they would pick the new fruit to make table wine. There are hundreds of varieties of wine grapes. Most grapes are used for table wine.

Jesse had just come from the livery barn and happened to catch a glimpse of her face as she turned to go into the hotel. He had never been so captivated. He immediately memorized her face. He noticed how her hair parted and divided her face, her beautiful face. Her hair was shoulder-length light brown, eyes would light up a room. What really caught his attention was her smile.

She walked into the hotel with an audience of young men watching her every movement. She was a lady, and yet she had a mischievous playful look about her. Jesse quickly took the rest of the rig off and took his belongings to the hotel to see if there was a room for the night. Then he would find a job to tie him over for the winter.

"Is there a room for rent anywhere in this town?" Jesse inquired.

"Sorry to say we're full this week. Let's see how long will you be staying in town?" the hotel manager asked.

"Hopefully, through the winter," Jesse replied.

"I know of one," the hotel manager said, scratching his head.

"Okay, what does it rent for?" Jesse asked.

"It's a trade out. Do some saddle bronc, wangle, ranch work and fix things and in exchange, the owner will board you and your stock until you decide to leave. It pays a dollar a day, also. She is good people," the manager said with a grin.

"It sounds good to me. Where is it?" Jesse asked knowing that the trade out would not be too difficult to handle.

"Go to the Lee Ranch east of here about a mile. You'll hit a grove of trees and then go southeast a quarter of a mile along Little Still Waters Creek," the manager explained.

"Thank you," Jesse said.

"Hey, who was the girl that came off the stage today?" Jesse asked.

"That would be Miss Alexandria Taylor. She is Megan Lee's niece, come to visit from Virginia," the manager said in low voice as to not attract attention.

"Thanks. Is she staying at the hotel?" Jesse's voice was getting softer also.

"Nope. She came in to visit some folks and then she goes to the ranch," The manager said, trying to match Jesse's tone.

"You mean she is staying at the ranch?" Jesse's voice became loud and attracted the attention of the other men who were on the other side of the doorway, and they began to laugh.

"That is where her aunt lives," the manager answered in the same loud voice.

"Sounds like you have eyes for Miss Alexandria," He said with a raised eyebrow.

"I don't even know her. I was just inquiring,"

Jesse could not hide the fact that his face was reddening.

"Well, you can inquire all you want when you get to the ranch." The innkeeper said with a snicker.

After Jesse had a hot bath, a shave, and time to rest Mariposa, Jesse once again saddled up and made plans to see about the job. The ride to the ranch was short but filled with thoughts about how to introduce himself to Mrs. Lee and Miss Alexandria.

Jesse for all this dealing with the inter-workings of ranch life back home and being able to speak to the ranch hands, he now had to deal with this odd feeling about meeting this girl for the first time.

He doesn't know why he was so concerned about this one girl. Maybe it was the fact that she was the first girl he ever wanted to meet. He was determined to meet her even though it was going to take some doing to overcome his shyness. He was drawn to her like no other girl.

"This is stupid. She is just a girl. I will introduce myself and that will be that," Jesse was summing up the courage to go to the front door. He took a deep breath and said a short prayer to ease his tension.

"Lord, give me the strength and the courage to go up to that door. I know that it is only a girl, but lord, did you have to make one so beautiful? I know we are here for a reason. Let me take this first step. I need you to give me the words to say. Amen."

Jesse took a deep breath, cleared his mind, and dismounted. He took off his hat, combed his hair, and went to the front door. He knocked gently, hoping it was Mrs. Lee and not Alexandria who answered the door. The door opened and it was Mrs. Lee. Jesse asked if she had a job for the winter.

"Young man, have you any experience doing ranch work?" She asked.

"Ma'am, I have been working a ranch since I was born. I was raised on my family's ranch in California. The ranch is located east of the Yosemite Valley in a place called the San Joaquin Valley in the town of Merced," Jesse answered

"What ranching skills do you have?" asked Mrs. Lee.

"I can bronc bust, work cattle, wrangle, and fix most things, and if need be, I can even cook."

"Good to know. We have a cook already. How are you at riding fence?" Mrs. Lee asked the last question to see how Jesse reacted, for no cowboy likes to work off his horse. Mending fence was considered a retirement chore given to those who were too old to do anything else.

"Ma'am, if that is what you need, then that is what I'll do." All ranch work is essential to make sure that the ranch runs efficiently," Jesse considered all work essential and not beneath hm.

"Do you drink?" Meg was still sizing him up.

"No ma'am. I could start tomorrow morning if you approve," With his hat in hand, keeping eye contact with Mrs. Lee, he smiled at her.

"I can use you. You can put your stuff in the main bunkhouse with the others. I will only take on four for the winter. You make the fourth. Senor Sanchez will be your foreman. Do exactly as he says. He is a good man." Mrs. Lee gave her okay.

"Yes ma'am, I will," Jesse kept eyes fixed on her.

"How old are you, and are you always so respectful?" Mrs. Lee was not used to having a young man be so polite.

"Yes ma'am, I am. My mother, aunts, and the nuns at school raised us to be this way. A gentleman is always a respectful man. There's no reason for disrespect. I am eighteen years old," Keeping his head up high and eyes on Mrs. Lee.

"Don't you want to know how much it pays?" She asked.

"Ma'am, whatever it is, I'm sure that it's fair enough," Jesse tipped his hat as he began to lead Mariposa to the bunk house.

"I think we are going to get along just fine. One question, what are you doing so far from home?" Jesse stopped and turned around.

"A man has the responsibility to do a man's job. I chose to leave home so I can come back a better man," Jesse did not want anyone to know his real reason for leaving home. It was a true enough answer, just not a complete one.

"I pay a dollar a day," Mrs. Lee said.

"Fair enough," said Jesse. He smiled and tipped his hat once again and then made his way to the bunkhouse.

Jesse knocked on the bunkhouse door and said, "My name is Jesse De La Souza, I was just hired on for the winter."

"I am Antonio J. Sanchez, I am the lead foreman. Over there is your bunk next to GW; glad to know you. We'll start at five in the morning. Eat all you want at breakfast, and we work until the job is done," Senor Sanchez sizing Jesse.

"Howdy, my name is Cody Williams, down from Kansas," Cody was a tall, slender cowpoke with reddish hair. He was about 17.

"Hey, they call me Travis John Johnson, TJ for short, and I am from everywhere; that is, I don't really know where I'm from originally. They tell me I was born in Texas. I've come down from Kansas, too." Travis is a young man around the age of 18 with dark hair, and of average height with a muscular build.

With the tip of his hat, George Washington Smith introduced himself. GW stood about six feet tall, in fact, everything about GW was big. He had a smile as big as his hat. "Hey, my name is George Washington Smith, but everyone calls me GW. I am from Oklahoma."

GW was a black/Cherokee cowboy. His dress was that of a quintessential cowboy, a button-up shirt of western design, a pair of faded jeans with cuffs over his boots, a red bandana, and a cowboy hat lifted high on his forehead. It gave him a rather friendly look. While the others just said hey, George Washington came to Jesse and shook his hand. Jess liked him right off.

Nowhere else in the country did blacks enjoy the same responsibilities and equality during the post-Civil War period than in the fraternity of cowboy in the Old West. Most post-Civil War cowboys were black. The pay for a cowboy was about one dollar a day. Most cowboys did not own their own stock due to the expense of it all. Their gear was loaned to them by the ranch where they worked. A loyalty pack between the cowboy and the ranch was made on a handshake. There was a no need to sign contracts. A cowboy's word was his bond. When he was hired it was understood that he 'rode for the brand,' which meant that he worked the ranch as if he owned part of it. For the most part, a cowboy only had his word.

"I'm glad to know all of you," Jesse made eye contact with each one of them as they introduced themselves.

"Hey Jesse, if you don't mind me telling you, what kind of an accent is that? Where did you say you're from?" Travis inquired.

"California," answered Jesse.

"What kind of cowboy are you? If you don't mind me asking, you carry a circle DLS brand on your rig and horse," asked Cody, he was looking out the window as Jesse rode up.

"If he is from California and lived on one ranch without leaving from season to season then that would make him a California Vaquero," answered Senor Sanchez.

"I am from Waco, Texas, so I am a Texas cowboy," answered Senor Sanchez.

"You sure do sound different," Cody added.

"My mother's family is from Espania, that is, originally from Spain. I was born and raised in a little town called Merced. That's in California."

"We're not making fun of you, mind you. Look like you might have some Indian blood and maybe some Mexican blood, too," Cody pointed out.

"It's just different, that's all. No offense," Cody added.

"No offense taken. I am proud of my heritage. A man's heritage doesn't make him a man. The way a man treats his fellow man makes him a man," Jesse answered.

"It's light out boys. We'll talk at first light," Senor Sanchez said in a fatherly voice which everyone obeyed without question. For the first time in a long time, Jesse closed both eyes and slept without thinking of the trail and the reason that brought him to this place in his life. He prayed for those he left at home, his horse, and for his new job. He slept deeply for the first time since he left home. Master Sheo would say that no one is ever left behind; if you remember them, they are always with you. He had just made some new friends and he was about the meet someone in the morning. Someone who he could not keep his mind off of. But, for now, it was sleep he needed and it came quickly.

{Ranching at the Lazy L}
The smell of coffee, bacon, eggs and fresh biscuits was all Jesse needed to wake him from his sleep. He remembered why he was here, and put on his work clothes and readied himself for the day. The first order of business was to pair up and divide the chores for the day.

"Eat up boys, you have a full day ahead of you," Sanchez going to each bunk and kicking the foot board. GW and Jesse were already awake and were getting their first cup of coffee.

"Eat all you want, but don't waste any of it. GW, you and Jesse head out to the south pasture area and bring in the stock closer to the ranch. Cody, you and TJ got fence today. GW and Jesse will switch off the next day," There were no arguments about the assignments. Mostly there were sounds of breakfast being shoved into hungry mouths.

Cody and Travis went to the north side of the property to finish mending fence so stock could be secured for the upcoming winter. GW and Jesse's job was to access the condition of the cattle, if need be care for them, and then bring them closer. Cowboys had many hats. There were no veterinarians nearby, so they had to look for signs of disease and, at times, aid in the delivery of a calf. Each man carried with him emergency items to aid another cowboy who was hurt on the prairie. Stitches were applied if called for, and many times without something to deaden the pain. Each cowboy carried a flask of whiskey, a few drinks and some grit. They would never show any signs of pain. They were required to 'cowboy up' and take it.

Mariposa spent the night in the open pasture, not needing to be tethered. All Jesse had to do was whistle for her and she would come. After the customary greeting, Jesse saddled her and gave her a cube of sugar. They were ready for the day. Mariposa was working horse and was happiest when she was working. Jesse kept his mind on his work, not wanting to disappoint Senior Sanchez.

"Say, what do you call her?" GW asked.

"Her name is Mariposa," Jesse said, patting her.

"What do you call your horse?" Jesse asked GW.

"I call her Rose, a right pretty name don't you think?" GW patting her and smiling with pride.

"I think so," Jesse was glad to know that GW liked his horse. He had a feeling they were going to good friends.

Sanchez shook hands with each one as they left to do the day's job. He felt it was important to let them know that they were not just hired hands, but a part of a team. He wanted them to feel like they could come to him for help. They were men all right but they were young men and still needed someone they could trust to talk to.

Sanchez shook Jesse's hand last. He could tell that this young man knew how to work by the feel of his hands. He knew that he had worked most of his life. Jesse's eyes revealed that he was someone who grew up much older than his years should show. His eyes were kind, but troubled. At the end of the day, Sanchez rode out to meet GW and Jesse.

"GW, can you excuse us? I need to talk with Jesse for a bit. Go see what's keeping them so long in mending that fence."

"Sure thing," With a tip of his hat and that huge smile, GW rode back to the ranch.

"Who taught you how to work?" Asked Sanchez.

"My family and the Vaqueros that lived on the ranch did," answered Jesse.

"Usually someone your age doesn't work as hard and as long as you do. You and GW make a good partnership," Sanchez pointed out.

"Men work, children play; I'm not a child," Jesse said being careful not to sound rude.

"I can see that," Sanchez said.

"You handle your horse well. I can see that you have spent a lot of time with her," Sanchez added.

"I have. She knows what I want sometimes before I even ask," Jesse patted her on the neck.

"It takes lots of years to train a horse to feel you," Sanchez looking at the brand on her.

"She was given to me when she was quite young. We have not been apart since. We spent a lot of time together. She is my friend not just my horse," Jesse stroking her mane with

Mariposa neighing in agreement.

"Animals don't usually let a person in like that. She must trust you for her to let you in," said Sanchez.

"She knows that I will protect her, and she will do the same for me. I talk to her, and I think she understands what I'm saying. I look at her body language and I can tell what she is thinking. I just sense it," Jesse felt that he may have said too much.

"She looks at you as if she understands you," Said Sanchez, who was noticing how Mariposa reacted to his touch.

"I can't explain it. I can just sense that she knows what I'm saying and can feel my thoughts. Does that make sense, or do you think I'm crazy?" Jesse looked directly at Sanchez to see if he would dismiss him. What he got was a man who listened and wanted to know more about him. Jesse had this feeling that he really cared about people and wanted to be his friend. Could he trust him enough to confide in him?

Senor Sanchez was old enough to be his father, but unlike his father, he talked with him and not at him. He listened and answered his questions. He was kind and genuine. He asked a lot of personal questions. It must be his way. Still, Jesse would wait until he knew without a doubt that he was really his friend before he opened up.

Senor Sanchez was a pretty good judge of character, and he knew that Jesse was different. He was not your typical cowhand drifter. He was educated, but something else was different. He had this feeling of familiarity about him. He was raised to be a gentleman, but works like a field hand and does not complain about the working conditions. He was a person he wanted to get to know better.   He would wait for Jesse to come to him.

Jesse was much too quiet for someone his age. Sanchez was sure that he was running from something but didn't know what it was. Educated, quiet, determined, mysterious, polite, gentle, kind, and well mannered, Jesse was different, and he wanted to know why he was here. What could he be running from? He didn't have the look of someone running from the law. He was running all right; but from what? Sanchez was interested in him maybe because he reminded him of himself at that age. He had a resemblance to someone he once knew in his youth.

"It's getting late. That's it for the today," Sanchez finally had enough for the day.

"Let's get home. We can start up again tomorrow. They are close enough for today. Don't you have someone to see?" Sanchez reminded Jesse of his appointment with Alex.

"How did you know?" Surprised Jesse asked.

"Every time that back door opened, you looked up, and you weren't looking for Mrs. Lee, it was Miss Alex, I think. I was your age once," Sanchez said with a smile.

"Is it that obvious?" Jesse dropped his head a bit.

"It is to me, and I think it is to her, also," Sanchez answered with a grin on his face.

"What do you mean?" Jesse answered back quickly.

"I think she has taken notice of you, also," Sanchez said back.

"How can you tell?" The look of surprise on Jesse's face indicated that his secret had been found out.

"I hear things, and I see things," Sanchez said in a playful tone.

"Go get cleaned up and don't forget your manners." Sanchez instructed Jesse as they left the job site.

After getting cleaned up and putting on his best bib and tucker, he made his way to the main house. Looking into the mirror several times before he left, he made sure that everything was in place. Stopping to rehearse what he was going to say, he heard a familiar voice.

"Relax, she won't bite you," Sanchez was coming up the path to report in and to let Mrs. Lee know that he was fixing to go get supplies from town. Jesse smiled nervously and began to rehearse again. He was looking down when he heard a voice coming from the open door.

"Who are you talking to?" A girl's voice came through the screen door.

It was Alex. Jesse looked up, she was in the doorway, and he was speechless. She just kept talking like she didn't notice his shock. Alex kept talking so they would not have that awkward silence between them. She looked at him and couldn't believe that he actually came to see her. She wanted to meet him from the moment she saw him. She noticed him when the stagecoach came in. She had to pretend as if she didn't notice him. It was not polite for a lady to stare at a stranger.

She was smitten by him and by the looks he gave her; she knew he liked her. She studied his face and looked into his dark brown eyes and noticed that he had long eyelashes and a well-defined jaw with a smile that lit his face up. She couldn't help but notice he had this boyish look on his face, which she found to be so attractive.

He was not your typical cowhand who often called on her. He was certainly different. She was used to having cowboys with no manners calling on her during her summer stays here at the ranch. Jesse stood tall and proud, but was unsure of himself.

"Hello, my name is Alexandria, but everyone here calls me Alex. You are not from around here, are you?" She asked, all the while looking at his face.

"Come in before the flies came in," Meg called out from the parlor. Meg never had known Alex to be so struck by someone.

"No, I'm not from around here. My family came from Spain, Texas, and now California. I was born in California," Jesse looked directly at her eyes and then back at the ground.

{Alexandria Taylor}
Alex always came during summer and went

home in the fall. She was from Virginia and had come to visit Aunt Meg since she was a little girl. Now she was hoping to stay and get her education here in town. Alex's parents wanted her to stay out west to help run the ranch. Alex's parents and Aunt Megan were in partnership in the ranch. Alex's parents worked for the U.S Government and had pulled some strings to let them have this ranch in the Indian Territories.

The U.S. Government needed someone to care for the Army issued horses and cattle the soldiers' stationed needed in the Indian and Oklahoma Territories. Supplies were usually brought in by the railroad. Since they were needed back in Virginia, the logical choice was to have the Lee's, Tom and Meagan, manage the ranch. Alex was no stranger to having young men call on her. She was a beautiful girl with soft brown hair and green eyes.

Back east, she had to be prim and proper. Here on the ranch, she could be herself and be a ranch girl. She enjoyed all the things that a ranch offered. Children out west knew how to have fun. Little girls back east had to be little ladies. Alex wanted to be free to ride and be out among the cattle and horses. She knew how to handle herself, and she has heard all the lines that the boys could give her. Jesse was different. He had a way about him that she had never encountered before. He was polite and respectful, yet he was no little boy. He unquestionably was a man. He was a gentleman.

"Are you going to invite him in, or do I have to do it?" Aunt Meg called out from the parlor.

"Oh yes, do come in," Alex regained her senses and opened the door just wide enough so Jesse could pass through almost face to face with her.

"Thank you," Jesse said without losing eye contact as he slowly slid past and touched her hand. He paused for a moment and took a deep breath, not wanting this time to pass. He was so close that they felt the warmth of each other's breath. He took in the scent of her perfume. Jesse was glad that brushed his teeth right before he came. A feeling came over him. He never had this feeling before. He wanted to kiss her. This was the first girl who ever made him feel this way, but he didn't know her, he wouldn't take what was not offered. She was the boss's niece and, most importantly a lady.

He thought of what Sister Maria had said about those feelings. It will lead to trouble, and Jesse had no idea the trouble his heart was going to get into. How could a feeling like this lead to trouble?

The moment was new for the both of them. Alex had had boyfriends, but she had not felt this way with any of them. For Jesse, this was something new, strange yet in a good way. Jesse had never seen this look on a girl before. She gave him this look that made his heart beat faster. He wanted to act on it, but it was new to him.

Aunt Meg was sewing when Jesse came in. The parlor was like his mom's, with pictures of the family and familiar nick knacks situated in strategic places. Sewing baskets were at the side of the sitting chairs, with each having a side table. On the tables were doilies and lamps. Everything was in its place. The room was cozy. The whole house smelled of fresh cookies, which added to the home feeling.

"You clean up well," Meg said, teasing him.

"Yes ma'am," Jesse replied.

"Sit down," Meg was looking down at her task. "How was your first day on the ranch?" Meg never looked up.

"It was fine, ma'am," Jesse replied.

"Okay, this is what we call a conversation, and that means you are going to have to say much more than 'Yes, ma'am."

"Yes ma'am," That was all Jesse could think to say.

"I hope you can get him to say more than that. I'm going to bed. Goodnight, you two," Aunt Meg turned toward Alex as she went upstairs, mouthing the words.
"He's a keeper."

"I know. Goodnight ma'am," Aunt Meg was teasing Jesse. She would not normally have gone to bed so early, but she knew that Alex could take care of herself. She had this feeling that she need not worry about this one. He was different, all right. He was a gentleman, and this place was in need of a few more. As she went upstairs, she wondered if there were more like him back home.

"I think she likes you," she said of Aunt Meg.

"I want to thank you two for allowing me to work here for the winter," Jesse said.

"I didn't even know you were hired until this morning," Alex said back.

"I have to confess to you," Jesse was about to explain when Alex interrupted him.

"This better not be a line. Mind you, I heard them all," she was hoping she was wrong. She was praying that this one be different. Her first feeling about Jesse had to be right. Please be right!

"As I was saying, I was about to confess that I knew you were here, and I wanted to meet you. I saw you as you came off the stage. I also knew that you were Mrs. Lee's niece," Jesse said without taking his eyes off of her. There was something about those eyes.

"Well, that is different. I was waiting to hear some lines about how you thought we were made for each other, and you were the best and could offer the world or some other nonsense," She was relieved that he was being truthful.

"I cannot offer you anything that your heart does not want," Jesse was talking from the heart and didn't know why it was so easy for him to do so. It was not like him to speak from the heart to someone new. Maybe she makes it easy because he sensed that she was different.

{Alex's thoughts}
You spoke from the heart. I knew you were not like the others. You really care about me, but how could you? You don't know me. I want to give my heart to you. Is it so wrong to feel this way at the beginning? Please don't break my heart. I want to give you something that I have never given anyone. Be the one I have been

looking for. She was looking beyond his eyes and into his heart. I am willing to give you my heart without really knowing you. I know you are the one.....

{Jesse's thoughts}
I cannot understand why I feel this way, I feel like I have known you forever. I have this stirring in my heart. I can't explain it. I don't want to explain it. I just want to feel it and never let it go. Please don't break my heart. I had a life time of hurt, but at this moment, it's gone. You have made all the hurt that I lived through disappear. You have filled my heart with something I was missing. I know you are the one. God, is she really the one? I pray that she does not hurt me. I have but only one heart to give. I will give it to you and pray that you accept it. Jesse had the strange feeling that someone was intervening on his behalf and was telling him that it was okay. Be yourself and let it happen. I have answered your prayers....

"Do you have the habit of speaking this way with girls you meet for the first time, or is this a line?" Alex wanted to believe, but she had to put up her guard to protect herself. She wanted to believe that he was for real.

I always tell the truth. I would like to ask your permission to call on you? "Jesse asked, hoping she would say yes.

"Okay, How about tomorrow afternoon after you get off work?" She knew his schedule and didn't want to waste time or for him to change his mind.

"I will pack a picnic, and we'll head down to Brush Creek, if that's okay with you?" She knew this was a spot where they could go to be alone. It was out of the way, so they would not be disturbed.

The day was not getting over fast enough for Jesse. His mind was on Alex. Senor Sanchez knew that he had his mind on something. He was trying to get the work done so he would have plenty of time to get cleaned up.

"Okay, we did enough for today. Let's pick the tools up and get cleaned up," Jesse did not hesitate and hurriedly picked everything up without saying anything.

"Slow down. She will wait for you," Jesse, was trying not to be so anxious. "Be yourself," Sanchez said in a fatherly tone.

"I am really nervous about this," Jesse was getting used to Sanchez giving him advice on such matters. His trust was growing, and he needed to ask someone about how to act with a girl.

"How you can tell if she wants you to hold her hand or kiss her?"

"She will let you know in her own way. I promise you, you will know. Just treat her with respect. And most importantly, be gentle with her. She is a young lady. If she is interested in you, you will know by the way she looks at you. There is no other look like the look that comes through the eyes of a woman who opens her heart to you," Sanchez was giving Jesse a life's lesson.

"Sus ojos son las ventanas del corazon," Sanchez said in Spanish to emphasis the lesson.

"Your eyes are the windows to your heart," Jesse repeated the words, and then he meditated on them until he finally understood the meaning Senor Sanchez wanted to get across. There was so much he didn't know. He wondered if she would notice his immaturity.

Then it occurred to him, what if she wanted him to kiss her? How to do it and for how long? He finally decided that it was not going to happen anyway so he didn't waste any more time thinking about it. He just wanted to make a good impression and take it from there.

{The Date}
With all that was on Jesse's mind, it was a

wonder that he remembered to bring the flowers that Sanchez suggested for Alex. He had never been on a date before. He had no idea what to do or say.

"Hi, these are for you," Jesse gave Alex the flowers as she opened the door.

"Thank you. They're beautiful," and with that, the date officially started.

It was a beautiful sunny day without a cloud in the sky; a perfect day for a ride. There was something about the smells and sounds of a ranch in late summer. The cut hay, the flagrance of summer wild flowers, and the mooing of cows brings good memories. The yelping of dogs, the cooing of doves in the hay loft, the constant clucking of chickens, the buzzing of flying insects, and even the scent of horse was enough to bring great memories. Jesse was now conscious of one new scent, the perfume that Alex wore. Scents usually bring up moments in our lives; this will be one day that he would always remember.

While walking to the barn, they asked questions to find out about each other without getting too personal. Jesse took notice of Alex's riding attire, which was different from what he was used to seeing on a woman. She wore a split skirt and high top riding boots with detachable spurs. Her hat almost matched his in style. She wore it just above her eyes, and with her hair being parted, it surrounded her face. She caught him looking at her and made a funny face. She had a playful spirit, and Jesse liked that. She was wearing an unusual small side arm.

"Say, what kind of gun is that?" Jesse asked.

"It's the latest thing. My dad got it for me when he was in Washington. It's a Smith and Wesson .38 double action hammer-less revolver," she pulled it out so Jesse could better see.

"It's really light and so small," Jesse was admiring the design and the weight of it compared to his Remingtons. It's so different. Where's the hammer?"

"The hammer is completely enclosed within the frame and is incapable of firing except by a long pull on the trigger. The reason is so you won't accidentally shoot yourself until you are ready to fire."

"I am impressed," he said, handing the revolver back to Alex.

"Which rig is yours?" Jesse asked.

"That one on the saddle rest, why?" He saw that the saddle was not a side saddle. Such was the reason for her wearing a split skirt. She rode just like a man. Good for her. She was not a sissy Sunday rider, but a ranch cowgirl.

"I was going to saddle your mount up for you," He was trying to be courteous.

"Why? Don't you think a girl is capable of doing it?"

"Can you?" Jesse wondered why she was questioning his intentions.

"I can do anything you can do. I have been saddling up my own horse ever since I could reach up and get onto a horse."

"Okay," Jesse gave in.

"Which horse is yours?" He asked.

"The Palomino Quarter horse in the third stall is mine. Isn't he beautiful?" Alex was beaming with affection.

"I've never seen one with a gold coat. His mane and tail are white. He sure stands out," Jesse was admiring Alex's horse.

"What's his name?" Jesse asks.

"Sam," answered Alex.

"My best friend is named Sam also. He and his family are the ones I'm going to visit in Missouri," Alex set her rig down, opened the stall, and lead Sam out. They greeted each other just like Jesse and Mariposa would have. Jesse watched Alex gently touch Sam's muzzle and slow hand motions over his face.

"Come and meet Sam," Alex motioned for Jesse to come over.

Jesse walked up to Sam slowly and extended his hand at waist level and waited for Sam to acknowledge him. With the initial touch over, he rubbed Sam's face and patted down his neck, making sure not to move too quickly.

"Let's get Mariposa and get them acquainted," Alex said.

"What breed is yours?" She asked.

"Mariposa is a Mustang. The breed was brought over from Spain when the Spanish Conquistadors came over," Jesse answered all the while stroking Sam.

"She is a beautiful mare," Alex had watched Jesse and Mariposa together with each seemingly enjoying each other's company. She is never tethered or hoppled. He spoke to her as if they were best of friends.

Jesse whistled for Mariposa to come into the barn. She came on the first whistle. Coming up to Jesse, they had to greet each other just like Alex and Sam did. Jesse brought her close to Sam so they could get used to their scents. With the greeting done, both horses were saddled.

"Where are we going?" asked Jesse.

"I am going to take you to my favorite place in the whole world," answered Alex.

"It should take about an hour or so to get there, but it will be worth the time," Alex had a twinkle in her eyes.

The ride was a time for each to get to know each other. Jesse found it easy to talk to Alex. He felt at ease with her. She was full of questions. The ride took a bit longer, but it seemed much less with all the questioning. The view of Brush Creek Falls and the pool below was well worth the time. Jesse had seen the Great Falls in the Yosemite Valley, and by those standards, this was just a drop off from the creek above. It didn't matter. He was here with Alex, and that alone was enough for him.

"This place is called Brush Creek Falls, and the pool is called The Blue Hole. It's very deep and cold once you go deep enough. I've tried to swim to the bottom, but I couldn't hold my breath long enough. The water is rather clear for this area. Most of our ponds are muddy with red sediment.

"Who owns this land around here?" Jesse asked.

"I don't really know. I rode out here with Aunt Meg and Senor Sanchez many times when I was much smaller. I'd go swimming and we would picnic here the whole afternoon," Alex answered.

"Do you think they own it?" Jesse asked.

"I don't know they don't come out here anymore. Anyway, I think this is the most peaceful place I know of," Alex was beaming with delight.

As soon as they dismounted, and having been raised on a ranch they knew to tend to their horses before they could turn their attention to themselves. After the horses were unsaddled and watered, they made camp using their gear to their advantage. Jesse was busy making sure the area was clear of concealed critters. He didn't mind the snakes. It was the ones he didn't see that bothered him. The saddle blankets were used to give distance between them and the grass, which was wet due to the mist of water splashing off the rocks into The Blue Hole. The saddles were used as back rests.

The food was unpacked, and then they sat quietly to take in the view of Brush Creek Falls.

"This has to be one of the prettiest places on Earth," Alex said.

"Someday I will have to show you Bridal Veil Falls in the Yosemite Valley," Jesse knew they were the most magnificent of all the waterfalls in Yosemite.

"I know there are prettier places elsewhere, but we are here and that's makes it the best place," Alex was content just to be here with Jesse.

"I can accept that," Jesse knew what she was saying, and it was the prettiest place on Earth. She was the reason for it.

As the day passed they talked about everything. They got to know more of each other, and it was effortlessly done, with no hidden agendas; just two people getting to know each other and feeling like they were supposed to be together. They walked the area, and Jesse spotted a pebble with an image of a girl's face on it.

"Look at this. It resembles a smiling girl's face," Jesse handed it to Alex.

"It sure does. Here, you keep it as a souvenir of our first date," Alex handed the pebble back to

Jesse. The day turned into early evening. They lost track of time, and it didn't matter to either one of them. It seemed like they had just gotten there and the day was ending all too soon.

"It's getting dark, and we need to start heading back. I don't want your aunt to worry," Jesse wanted to do the right thing, but he also didn't want the time with Alex to end.

"I know you're right. We can do this again tomorrow if you want," Alex was hoping he didn't think it too forward of her to ask for another date.

"Tomorrow would be fine," Jesse was happy to know that she wanted to see him again. He was what she wanted him to be, and she wanted to end the date in a memorable way. They got all their belongings together and saddled the horses. They took a last look at Brush Creek Falls as the last of the sunlight skipped across the pool. It was perfect.

Alex and Jesse were standing next to each other and turned to face each other. They were inches apart, just like the first time they met at the back porch. Close enough to feel the warmth of their breath. The intoxicating sounds of the falls and the aroma of the lavender filled their senses.

The last of the twilight gave way to moonlight.

The scene was set to perfection. Alex gazed into Jess's eyes, and without saying what she wanted, she let her eyes tell him that it was okay to kiss her. Jesse saw the look in her eyes, and it dawned on him that Senor Sanchez was right. Look for the eyes that speak from the heart and you will know.

! Sus ojos son las ventanas del corazon! He didn't have to think about it. He didn't hesitate; he just knew what he was supposed to do. He took what she offered and kissed her softly and she kissed him back. The eyes are the windows to the heart were Jesse's last thought before he kissed her again and again.

Both were lost in their world; absorbed with their thoughts. They backed away and decided it was not enough, so they kissed several more times and held each other in silence, knowing they had found what they were looking for. From this moment on, they knew what their kiss meant. They were in love. Jesse didn't need anyone to tell him what he felt.

"We better go," Jesse said, breaking the silence.

"I don't want to go, but I did promise your aunt that I would take care of you," Jesse was a man of his word and he was afraid of what might happen if they stayed any longer. He respected her, so he must do the honorable thing and take her home.

"I know," Alex replied in a disappointing tone.

"We can do this tomorrow, right?" Alex was hoping that there was a "yes" coming.

"Yes, and this time let's start earlier," Jesse was hoping she wanted to see him again.

"Now, let's mount up and get on our way before it gets too late. I don't want anyone to start rumors about you," Jesse was looking after her reputation.

He is looking after my reputation. He must care for me. I knew he was different; he wants me to be safe. I know that he is the one. I knew it at the moment I saw him. And now after we kissed, I gave him my heart. Alex was sure of her decision, everything in her world was wonderful.

The ride home was filled with laughter, and more plans were made for the coming days. It was good that Mariposa and Sam knew where home was because Jesse and Alex were lost to each other. The ride soon ended and Jesse took her mount and told her that he would tend to her. They looked at each other one last time.

The back door opened, and Aunt Meg told them

that it was getting late, "Someone say goodnight," That was all that was needed, Jesse leaned close to Alex and softly kissed her with slight squeeze of her hand to let her know that he was going.

The horses were taken to the barn and all the necessary caring for them done. This night, Mariposa was kept inside. Jesse went to the bunk house and called it a night. Five am. Just seven hours away. It didn't take much time for him to drift off to sleep. He had a good day, the best day he had ever had. He was thankful. Just before he was asleep, he gave thanks to the one. Jesse also gave a special prayer to the ones who were not there, all his family and to his two friends who were always on his mind.

Senor Sanchez kept quiet when Jesse came into the bunk house. He would wait until the morning to see how things went. He wanted Jesse to enjoy this night with his thoughts. By the way he came in; he sensed that the date went well. Morning is coming soon enough. Antonio had his own thoughts he was trying to keep them from coming up. As he drifted back to sleep, the thought of someone from his past emerged. He tried to keep her hidden deep in his heart.

The events of the past he trying to escape from came out to haunt him once again. The love he didn't want to forget but tried to forget came to him. He drifted in and out of sleep. Antonio gave in to the memories and dreamed of her. He was back with the woman he loved, and life was good. Even though she was just there for the night, he welcomed her. The pain his heart held was lessened. Reality would come at first light.

{The next morning}
The sound of roosters brought in the beginning of the new day. Cody and TJ were a little slow in getting up, so Senor Sanchez helped them by getting morning water buckets and reminded them that he was not their mother. The cold water was enough to wake even the soundest sleeper. They shot out of bed and got dressed quickly. The morning breakfast was being served.

"Good morning everyone, I hope you all had a good night's sleep. It's going to be a busy day. Jesse, you and GW have milking duty today. TJ and Cody, you have firewood cutting for the morning, and then break in two new mounts. Jesse, after you get done milking, go clear the loft of varmints. GW, after milking, come find me. We have some supplies in town to fetch. Everyone understand your duties today?" Sanchez cupped his right ear, which meant for the boys to acknowledge him.

Everyone said "Yes, sir," so the day began.

TJ and Cody couldn't keep from poking fun at Jesse about last night date. Jesse's face grew red and he said nothing. Senor Sanchez knew it would be a matter of time before the kidding would get to Jesse, so he ended it.

"Ah, we're funning with you. We meant no harm," they apologized for their playful harassment.

"That's okay. I guess I deserved that since I was late getting back in last night," Jesse was trying to ease the embarrassment.

"Okay, give up the story," Cody wanted to know details about the date.

"What story?" Jesse knew what they wanted. He sipped his coffee.

"Give it up," TJ was trying to get a rise out of Jesse by baiting him.

"There is nothing to say. We rode out to Brush Creek Falls and had a picnic. Nothing else happened," at this point, Jesse was trying not to get upset with them by their insinuations.

"I believe boys that will be enough of that," Senor Sanchez wanted to get to work, and he didn't want the conversation to get out of hand.

"Aren't you going to say anything?" Jesse asked GW.

"Nope," GW answered.

"Why?" Jesse was curious why he didn't want in the fun.

"What a man does is his business. I think you treated her with respect, and nothing has to be said. Those two are boys with stupid on their minds. That's all I have to say about it," GW was getting ready for the day, he respected Jesse.

"Okay, let's get to work. I need all of you tomorrow out on the range picking up strays and moving them to the enclosures. GW, change with Jesse this afternoon. We'll going into town to get supplies," Sanchez was a man of little words, but what he said, he meant. The men respected him and never gave him any trouble about what he assigned them.

"Let's get going. We have a full day today, and I want to finish before the moon comes up," The boys knew what that meant and quickly got ready for the day. The afternoon ride into town was short, but long enough for Sanchez to visit with Jesse about his date last night.

"You handled yourself well this morning,"

Sanchez started the conversation.

"They meant no harm. They were just funning me," Jesse didn't want Sanchez to know that it bothered him.

"Now listen, if we are going to trust each other, we need to tell the truth," Sanchez was laying the ground work for a trusting relationship.

"Yes sir," Jesse knew that he was caught, not in a lie, but not telling the whole truth.

"How you answered it says a lot about your character," Sanchez was trying to let Jesse know that if you care about someone you don't go blabbing out the things that go on between a man and a woman.

"I respect her," Jesse was looking directly into Sanchez's eyes.

"I know, but here's some truth that I want you to think about. I have known that child since she was born. Knowing her, I suspect that she will keep her wits about her. She can take care of herself. I never had any daughters of my own, so I look at her as my own daughter, understand?" Sanchez tone changed.

"Yes sir," Jesse knew the tone and the underlying meaning of what Senor Sanchez was saying. He cares about her like I do.

"By the little that I know of you, I can tell that you will respect her in all things. I also know that you are different from the other boys. You are mature for your age. Someday, when you are ready, I would like to know more about you, okay?"

"Yes sir," Jesse realized that Sanchez was a caring man. He wanted the best for Alex and now he cared enough to want to get to know him.

The general store had all the Sanchez ordered, and the two of them headed back to the ranch. They made a stop at the Army post to let the commander know the new mounts would be ready in a week or two. Their last stop was at the furrier's to make sure he knew what to come out.

"Senor Sanchez, can I ask you some questions?" Jesse asked.

"Yes," Sanchez looked directly at Jesse.

"You really care about Alex, don't you?" Jesse asked.

"Like she was my own," answered Sanchez without hesitation.

"I do too." Jesse said. He gave her something that he had never given before, his heart. And with that gift, he gave his love and finally understood what it meant to love someone.

"Can I ask you another question?" Jesse asked.

"You don't have to keep asking me if you can ask another question every time you want to ask me a question. Okay," Sanchez poked Jesse in fun.

"Where is home for you?" Jesse asked. It was getting easier asking questions.

"I was born and raised in Waco, Texas. I left there when I was not much older than you," Sanchez answer was filled with underlying tone of sadness.

"Why did you leave there?" Jesse was curious as to why he left his home at such a young age.

"I had nothing to keep me there," Sanchez answered.

"I'm not getting too personal, am I?" Jesse wanted to know these things but he also wanted to be respectful of his privacy.

"I have given you permission to ask whatever you like," answered Sanchez.

"Okay," The okay by Jesse was a little hesitant. He didn't really want anyone to know why he came out this way. But, he gave his word. The worth of a man is whether his word is his bond. Jesse always told the truth, and as much as this might be painful, he will honor his word.

"What did you mean, nothing was keeping you there?" Jesse asked the question but he had a quick thought that maybe he overstepped his boundary.

"I am going to tell you something that only two others know," Sanchez's voice was filled with emotion. He knew this young man was sensitive enough to hear what he had to say.

Jesse understood the importance of this time with Senor Sanchez. The two were sharing something from the heart, and the relationship between the two was changing. Jesse so much wanted this to be a trust bond that he could not have with his father. He felt he could trust Sanchez with the innermost thoughts and his pain. He wanted to have a father/son relationship with Senor Sanchez.

"I left my home because of a young girl not much older than you," Sanchez had Jesse's full attention.

"Not just any girl, she was the love of my life," He was trying not to let the emotions come up.

"Why did you leave, if she was the love of your life?" Jesse was not understanding Sanchez's choice.

"I had no choice. Her family thought I was not good enough for her. Leaving brokenhearted was not what I wanted to do," Sanchez was picturing her in his mind.

"Why did you leave?" Jesse asked the question again, for he was not given an answer that he could understand.

"Her family came from the old country, and they believed it was the family's right to arrange their children marriages. They decided that it was best for her to be given to someone who they thought was best for her." Sanchez had flash images of his love.

"She let them do that?" Jesse was having trouble understanding what he was being told. He understood the words, but he couldn't understand leaving someone you loved behind.

"She was raised to be obedient to her parents and regardless of her feelings, she obeyed," Sanchez was reliving the last he spent with her.

"Why did you not just take her if you loved her?" Jesse just couldn't understand him leaving her.

"I had to honor her choice, and I had to think of my parent's situation in all this," Sanchez was beginning to form tears. He quickly wiped them away.

"How could you live with the knowledge that your love was taken away from you? Jesse shook his head. He could not believe that Sanchez would let that happen.

"Sometimes, you just have to do things. I thought with my head and not my heart. I have regretted that decision ever since. I should have followed my heart," Sanchez was heavy hearted and the memories were coming back. He looked away for a bit and turned back to Jesse.

"I have dated others, but it was not the same. I hope that you never go through this. I have tried to forget her, but my heart won't let her go. Do you believe in God, Jesse?" Sanchez asked.

"Yes," Jesse was surprised that he would ask.

"I prayed that he would take that pain away," Sanchez opening up even more deeply.

"Did he?" Jesse asked in a low hushed voice.

"No. What I think he was trying to tell me was to use this pain to strengthen myself for other things," Sanchez was trying to make sense of it himself.

"What I have found out from all this, is that this was truly love, for she has not been absent from my heart or head since I left," Sanchez placing his hand over his heart.

"Jesse, what do you pray for?" Sanchez wanted to find out more of what Jesse believed in.

"I pray mostly for strength and courage and, of course, for those that I care for,"
Jesse pointing up to the sky indicating his God.

"Do you have any regrets about what happened?" Jesse was still trying to understand Sanchez's feelings.

"I regret the choice I made to honor her choice. I should have followed my heart and taken her with me," Sanchez placed his hand over his heart.

"Do you know where she is?" Jesse hanging onto Sanchez's every word.

"I heard that she was taken to San Francisco, California. I can still see her face. You know, you never forget the love of your life, and the worst part is that you never forgive yourself for not following your heart," this brought a smile to his face. He still remembered the details of her face.

Sanchez was still thinking about her when they reached the ranch. Even though it had been many years, the pain was still very much there. For this reason, he had not spoken about her because he hid the pain deep for fear that the pain would resurface like it did today. He took the chance and failed. He was feeling just like it happened today. Sanchez needed to open up to Jesse so Jesse would do the same to him. Sanchez had the feeling that Jesse was hiding something, something very painful, and he wanted to help him. He wanted Jesse to release his pain. He knew all too well the effects of the hurt. He rested his left hand on Jesse's shoulder.

"We'll talk more about this later, but for now, let's get back to work," Sanchez patted Jesse's shoulder.

Alex was up as early as the boys and busying herself with her chores. Aunt Meg was thankful for her company. Autumn was approaching, and the ranch was getting ready for the upcoming winter. Alex was singing when Aunt Meg came into the barn. She knew the reason for her singing. She was happy that someone had made her happy. She cared for Alex as if she were her own.

Ever since her husband's death, Meg had worked the ranch along with Sanchez. She couldn't leave it. It would be like leaving him. Tom was buried on the property. She was invited to go back east to live with her sister, but the time never seemed right to leave. It had been several years since he passed away. This was their home, and she couldn't leave her home, but she knew that one day she couldn't keep up with it all. Until then, she would stay and keep the dream alive for Tom.

"I know why you're singing.........," Aunt Meg teased Alex. Meg had never seen Alex so happy. She had had boyfriends before, but this was different. She was different. She was singing without a care in her life. Her smile said it all.

"That must have been some date last night?" Meg said.

"It was!" Alex's eyes were fixed looking inwardly.

"Okay, let's have it," Aunt Meg wanted details.

"Promised not to laugh?" Alex made a cross sign on her own heart.

"I always do," Meg was smiling.

"It was perfect," her face told the story before any details were given.

"Okay, out with it." Aunt Meg was wanting details.

"I packed a picnic, and we rode out to Brush Creek Falls and talked. We got to know each other. We shared our dislikes, and even our dreams," Alex was beaming with joy.

"You mean you got that one to talk about his dreams?" Meg asked.

"I didn't think he could say anything but, yes ma'am. He had a lot to say," Alex interrupted Aunt Meg.

"You know he is from California, and he wants to someday own a ranch and vineyard. But first he wants to go to a university and study," Alex talking so fast that Aunt Meg couldn't understand her.

"Study what?" Meg asked.

"I don't know. I was busy looking at his eyes. I didn't pay much attention to what he was saying at the point," Alex grinning from ear to ear.

I'm sure he will do what all men want to do and that is ranch and stuff. You know he didn't say much about his parents," Alex was thinking on her statement.

"Go on," Meg was looking for more details.

"As the day was ending, the most beautiful moon rose. The moonlight came across the water, and that's when he kissed me," Alex closed her eyes and twirled once around.

"It was the most romantic kiss I've ever had," Alex held her arms across her chest and all the while keeping her eyes closed.

"He was a gentleman the entire time, so much so that he was even concerned with my reputation and brought me home before it got too late," Alex opened her eyes and looked at Aunt Meg.

"He didn't want anything else?" Aunt Meg was making sure that nothing else went on.

"No, he was so concerned about my well-being and what others would think about me that he ended the date and brought me home. We made plans to go out again. It is okay isn't it? I mean, you don't need me for anything do you?" Alex looked directly at Aunt Meg waiting for the okay.

"No, I will get Senor Sanchez to help me while

you two are off making eyes at each other," Aunt Meg those made funny eyes to give emphasis to her statement.

The rest of the day was spent finishing their chores and, of course, retelling the entire date. Meg was glad Jesse had come to stay for a while. She didn't want to think what would happen when he left next spring.

She was thinking about how Alex would feel. Maybe Jesse would change his plans and stay. She had to busy herself and not think about what the future would bring. At this moment, Jesse was bringing happiness to her niece, and that was all she was really thinking of.

Meg watched Alex dance around the barn, singing and smiling. What was more important in life than love and happiness? With all the things you can possess, the things that matter most are what resides in your heart and the relationships you cultivate. The riches of a person are not what he can buy or obtain, but the love that is given and returned. Riches are stored in the heart.

{The weekend}
Weekends on the ranch were like any other work day, except Aunt Meg prepared lunch in a picnic atmosphere and the work day ended at noon. The men usually had the rest of the day off and

Sundays until late afternoon. There wasn't really anytime off on the ranch. Everyone had their chores to do before lunch was served, and usually the men were seated first. Custom dictated that those who did the work got fed first.

Jesse understood this ranch custom, but he never would adhere to it. At home, he waited until everyone was served and seated, including the women, and then he would serve himself. His first weekend on Mrs. Lee's ranch, he stayed true to what he believed and did the same as if he were home.

"Hey, Jesse, you don't have to wait on the women folk. Sit down and get to eating," TJ called out with a mouthful of chicken.

"It's okay. They expect you to eat first," Cody yelled with corn bread spitting out of his mouth.

"I will wait until the women are seated," Jesse answered.

"Why?" TJ asked.

"It is a matter of courtesy and manners," answered Jesse.

"It's supposed to be this way," TJ answered.

"Manners are manners, wherever you are," Jesse said.

Jesse, you are so right, I am with you on this," GW waited until the ladies were seated and took his place across from Alex. Jesse was thankful that GW had the same respect and manners as he did. They were becoming the best of friends. Jesse needed a friend his own age to talk to. GW was in need of a friend, too.

Aunt Meg and Alex listened in and thought Jesse was right. Jesse and GW waited until all the women were seated and then took their seats. His place was, next to Alex. Senor Sanchez was impressed by Jesse's answer to Cody and TJ. He was going to find out more about this young man.

The women were equally impressed and liked the fact that he always stood up as they got up. "Where did he learn to be so mannerly? Aunt Meg's thought. This place needed more like him. After lunch, everyone helped cleared the tables. The men rode into town to see what they could find. They were looking for a Bit House to bend and elbow or two.

"Jesse?" Sanchez called out and motioned for him to come to see him.

"You made an impression on Mrs. Lee."

"It was the way it was supposed to be," Jesse was wondering why it was hard to understand.

"That is not why I called you over. Do you feel comfortable enough to tell me why you are so far from home?"

"Someday, not yet, but soon," Jesse lowered his eyes, not wanting to make eye contact with Sanchez. He wanted to tell, but he needed more time to sort it out for himself.

"Okay, I'm here if you want to talk," Sanchez put his arms around Jesse in a fatherly embrace. At first, Jesse wanted to pull away, and then he found comfort in it. Jesse looked at Sanchez and told him it would be soon.

Alex watched Jesse and Senor Sanchez and was curious to see them interact. She noticed that Jesse acted like a son to a father more than a ranch hand to his boss. She found that to be very interesting. She never saw Senor Sanchez act so concerned about someone, especially someone who worked at the ranch. She decided it was a personal thing between them, and Jesse would tell her if there was something to it, or would he?

Alex waited behind the oak tree to jump out at Jesse. She was in a particularly playful mood and wanted to act silly with him. As planned, he went past, and she pounced like a cat onto Jesse's back. Jesse was glad for the mood change from the serious one he and Sanchez just had.

He wanted nothing but to forget his past and concentrate on the present and a possible future with Alex. Being with her was all he wanted, and his every waking thought was on her. He could not remember a happier time. Once they were out of everyone's sight, they slowed down and began to walk side by side. Nothing was said. They enjoyed the silence between them. It was not an awkward silence. It was the kind in which they could sense the others thoughts.

Jesse touched her hand and she responded by taking hold of it. He smiled, and without looking at her, he knew she was smiling back. They found themselves in the grove of Shumard oak trees where they stopped to rest. They made sure that the vegetation growing up the trunk was Virginia creeper and not poison ivy. Jesse recited the phrase, "Leaves of three let it be."

After making sure it was all right, Jesse sat against the tree trunk. Alex sat on his lap and wrapped her arms around his neck. Jesse was new to this, so he just looked at her and said nothing. Surely she could feel the pounding of his heart.

Alex lowered her head onto his shoulder and sighed. It was not a sigh that something was wrong; it was a sigh of comfort. Alex rested in that position for a few minutes and then looked up. The warmth of that touch gave way to kissing. Several minutes later, they stopped, and she pulled away. Jesse caught his breath and looked into her eyes. He knew that his heart was not his own. He thought about it, and wondered if she felt the same.

"Jesse, will you tell me the truth about something?" Alex asked.

"I will always tell you the truth," answered Jesse, still looking into her eyes. His mind raced with what the next question was going to be and to what extent he was going to let her into his past.

"How do you feel about me?"

"I don't understand," answered Jesse.

"Ask the question another way." He was hoping it was a general question. Then it hit him she wanted to know his intentions for her.

"It was a direct question, but I will say it this way. When you are not with me and you think about me, and you do think about me don't you?" Alex was fishing for an answer.

Jesse nodded his head to answer yes. Jesse thought to himself, if it was this way for a girl to be so insecure about things. It was all new to him. To him, once there was an understanding, it was done. A woman must have to be told many times before they felt secure about it. He would be patient and reassure her when asked.

"How do I make you feel when you think about me?" She finally said, and awaited his answer. She put her heart out there and hoped it came back whole.

Jesse thought about it. It was taking too long for Alex, and she knew that the answer was not going to be the one she was hoping for. She dropped her head and a tear formed when Jesse finally spoke.

"I think about you when I go to sleep, when I wake up, at breakfast and when I'm working. I never stop thinking about you. You are all I think about. I have this feeling deep down in my gut. I can't explain it. I want to be near you every moment of the day. When we kiss, all I can think about is that I am the luckiest person in the world. I don't want to ever leave. I have never had this feeling before in my life. All I want to do is be near you."

"Jesse, it sounds like you...," Alex wanted him to

say the words, those words that every girl wants to hear. She wanted to make sure he was feeling the same as she felt.

"If this is the way love feels, then Alex, I love you. I can't begin to tell you how you make me feel. You're beautiful and not just to look at but, inside you're beautiful." With the words spoken he felt closer to her. Most importantly, Alex heard the words she wanted to hear. He finally understood her need to hear them.

His thoughts went back to Sister Maria and understanding what she was saying; that love is powerful emotion. How could love be so dangerous? It feels good. How can love be a dangerous thing?

"Jesse looked at her, leaned closer, kissed her gently and said, "I looked into your eyes and saw your heart. I know how you feel."

"Well, I am going to tell you anyway. I love you," she hugged him and held him without saying anything else.

"I think we need to be getting back," Jesse thoughts were again on Alex, and he wanted only the best for her.

"Let's get the horses and go to The Blue Hole and go swimming before it gets too late," Alex wanted just to spend time with Jesse.

"That sounds great," Jesse had a similar idea, which was to be alone with her. It didn't matter where. He was focused on her. He found himself looking at her, studying her face and the way she made those funny expressions.

He watched Alex and how she moved when she walked. She had a rhythm to her. Everything about her mesmerized him. She had a way of expressing herself through her eyes and facial expression. She was the prettiest girl he had ever seen. She made him laugh, and not just inside. He laughed out load for the first time in his life.

He was tired of being alone. He needed her. He needed someone to share his thoughts with. His life made sense now, and for the first time in his life, he was content. His thoughts were not of himself, but always of her. What a wonderful feeling this feeling of love was. What could be so wrong about loving someone?

"Tony, can you help me later this afternoon?" Meg asked Sanchez before he left the picnic area. When no one was around, she used his first name. They were friends, close friends.

"Meg, I know that tone. What's on your mind?"

"I want to discuss something with you," Meg needed to know more of Jesse.

"Is that thing named Jesse?" Sanchez placed his hand on her shoulder.

"It's just one of the things," Meg's voice was filled with sadness.

"I should ride into town just to make sure they get into too much trouble. I'll be back in an hour or so, and then we can visit," Tony puts his hand on Meg's hand.

"You better go. You don't want trouble finding those kids." Megan gave Tony a hug. Tony knew when she was troubled. He could read her very well.

Tom Lee and Antonio (Tony) Sanchez were the best of friends and together had shared many adventures coming from New Mexico. Tony was Tom's best man at the wedding. When Tom knew he was dying from small pox, he asked Tony to watch over Meg. He knew he would be the person he could trust to watch over her. Tom knew that Tony cared for her very much. Tom was not a jealous person, especially with Tony, because he knew he was an honorable man.

Tony was a trusted friend and godfather to their

only child. Sarah died of the small pox the year before. She was only five years-old. Tom and Megan could not have more children. After the small pox epidemic was over, Megan looked after Alexandria, their niece, as her own. She came out during the summers to visit and help with the ranch. It was like having Sarah there in her place. She was at peace with it.

The boys found the saloons and had a beer at each of them. It was getting late in the afternoon, they decided one more drink for the road and walked into the last saloon on the street. The men at the bar stopped drinking when GW entered.

"Hey you, what the hell do you think you're doing?" An obvious drunk said pointing at GW.

"I've come in to get a drink," GW smiled. He was not looking for any kind of confrontation, so he tried to defuse the moment.

"We don't serve your kind here!"

"We'll be gone as soon as my partners and I get a drink. We're not looking for any trouble," Cody said. The drunk was looking for trouble. He drew his gun and pointed it at GW. Sanchez walked into the saloon at that moment.

"You don't want to do that, mister," Sanchez had

his gun out and ready to end this. Cody, TJ, and GW stood their ground. The other men moved from harm's way.

"This is none of your concern. We don't serve his kind here," The drunk took another drink of whiskey and slammed the shot glass on the bar for effect.

"You have two choices. Holster it or die trying to use it. As I can tell, you are too drunk to hit anything," Sanchez was only a few feet from the man.

"What are they to you anyway? They are trash for being with that Indian buffalo!" said the drunk, using a crude slang term for Indian and black mixed bloods.

"He is more of a man than you. I will protect all of them like they were my own. I don't have all night! I'm losing my patience. What's it going to be, live or die?" With this, Sanchez cocked the colt and was slowly squeezing the trigger.

The drunk looked around to see if any of his friends were going to help. None did. He dropped his revolver on the bar and backed away from it. The bar keeper picked it up and nodded his head to Sanchez. Sanchez knew the bar keep and nodded back.

"Okay, boys, looks like you need to get back to the ranch," Sanchez pointed his colt at the drunk until the boys left. They apologized to Sanchez and thanked him for bailing them out.

"Why, it was not your doing. Next time, just back out. There are too many fools out there, and I may not be there next time to take care of it. Now, you all get back to the ranch and say nothing to Mrs. Lee. I don't want her to worry about you."

"Yes sir," they said.

Sanchez followed them back to the ranch to make sure trouble did not follow them. Back at the ranch, he went to the barn to make sure they put up their horses making sure that all the gates were securely latched. Meg met him at the barn.

"Tony, I want to talk to you about Jesse," Meg's tone was serious.

"Okay, after I'm finished here. Give me about an hour or so?" Tony answered without looking at her.

"Okay, I'll make coffee," He went to the house two hours later and met Meg on the porch. She was glad to see him and gave him a hug.

"I need to know some things about Jesse. You seem to know him best. Where does he come from? Who is his family? Why...," Meg was talking a mile a minute.

Tony stopped Meg in mid-sentence. "Wait a minute, one question at a time. I know just as much as you do."

"I only ask because I am looking after Alex's welfare."

"So am I," Tony was calm and wanted Meg to follow his lead.

"I have been talking to him, and he will let me know all about him when he is ready. He is one that I can trust with Alex. I sense that he really cares about her. And besides, it isn't up to us, is it?" Tony rubbed Meg's arm and smiling.

"I know. I just want her to be happy," Meg patted Tony's arm in return.

"Is she not happy?" Through his observations, Alex was the happiest that he had ever seen her.

"I just don't want her to get hurt," Meg was concern that maybe they were moving too quickly in their relationship.

"I think we should let those two alone and let

them get to know each other. We need to stay out of it. Alex is a smart girl."

"Can you find out more about him?" Meg asked.

"I will, and I bet you that he is what he seems to be. There is something so familiar about him," Tony smiled to reassure Meg.

"I know I would feel better if I knew more," Meg was still being the mother hen.

"I miss Tom," Meg's voice was soft and filled with sadness.

"I miss him too, Meg."

"I know he wanted me to keep up this ranch, but I don't know how long I can do this."

"We can do this for as long as you want to. You know I promised Tom I would look after you."

"I know, but aren't you lonely?" Meg's wanted Tony to be happy.

"I have all of this to care for, and besides, there will be time for all that later," That was Tony's typical answer to that particular question.

"With you; it is always later," Meg smiled again. Tony left Meg with that answer and went on his customary ride by himself. For the most part, he kept this part of his life hidden. He was missing her. There was a void in his heart even after all the years that have passed. Tony also had feelings for Meg, but he kept this from her. He felt that it has not been long enough to tell her about it. He wanted Meg to feel the same, but that will come with time, maybe. His feelings for Meg and the memory of his lost love complicated things.

After Tony left, Meg's thoughts turned to Tom. All three were the best of friends, she had wanted Tony to ask her out once upon a time before Tom did. Tony was slow to show any interest in her, so when Tom asked her, she accepted.

Meg later found out the reason why Tony never asked her. She felt sorry for Tony because of the way it turned out. Tony was the best friend Tom ever had, and Meg too, for that matter. Megan had feelings for Tony but thought it was due to their friendship over the years. Meg didn't want to complicate their friendship, so she never talked to him about her feelings.

{The Blue Hole}
The temperature was hot with the humidity just as high. The water was refreshing. Alex took off her riding skirt and top shirt and dove right in. She had no inhibitions about taking off her

clothes in front of Jesse. She felt comfortable and knew he would not take advantage of the situation or think any less of her.

"Jesse, you are just going to have to loosen up a bit and jump in." Alex was already next to the falls trying to urge Jesse to come in.

"I am not going to take my pants off." Jesse was self-conscious about the fact that she wanted him to take them off.

"Don't be silly, I seen lots of boys with their underpants on. I don't know about how California boys do it, but out here, we take off our pants and shirts before we jump in, not after," Alex was grinning from ear to ear she waited for him to take those pants off.

"Turn around first," Jesse did not want to admit it, but he was shy, maybe too shy for his own good. Alex turned around when Jesse began to take his pants off, Alex turned back around just to tease him.

"It looks like someone needs a tan down there!" She yelled out.

Jesse, caught with his pants half off, hurried to pull them back up and fell into the water. Alex laughed. Jesse was red with embarrassment but later thought it was pretty funny himself.

"You're going to have to laugh at yourself more," Alex trying to get him to loosen up and not to be so concerned about what the others think. She was here because she wanted to be. She was in love and wanted them to enjoy all the little things that brought joy to life. She wanted Jesse to not be so serious all the time. She didn't understand why he was always so uptight about what everyone was thinking. She wanted to know more of his parents, family, and his growing up in California. He didn't talk about them much. She wanted to get a sense of who he was, but she would wait until he decided to tell her.

"This feels great, not as cold as the places I swam in before," Jesse was making reference to the lakes and creeks in Merced. Those pools were filled with snow melt water from the spring thaws.

"Aren't you going to take off your shirt?" Alex asked.

"Yea, sure," Jesse hesitated and finally took it off.

"Let's swim under the falls. I want to show you something," Alex swam to where the falls were hitting the pool, submerged herself, and swam under the falls. An opening to a cave was hidden just under the lip of the pool. Cattails and bamboo grew on each side of the falls. Jesse followed and surfaced at the opening of a cave barely large enough to fit through. Alex got out of the water with Jesse not too far behind her. She didn't mind that Jesse saw her in her underwear. He liked that about her.

"I want to show you something. I found them years ago. No one believes me that they are here," Alex didn't want to say much about it and wanted Jesse to see for himself.

"What is it?" Jesse's eyes were still adjusting to the darkness.

"Wait a few minutes. Don't go any further until you can see," the sun's rays penetrated from cracks in the rock wall where avalanches had sealed both ends of the cavern. Sunlight from the underwater cave opening gave additional light. Jesse waited for his eyes to adjust to the faint light, and then he saw them.
There were dozens of them. They looked like buffalo except they had flat horns across the top of their heads and were pointed sideways. Jesse couldn't believe his eyes.

"How did they get here, and why did they die here?" Alex asked.

"That's incredible. No one believes you?" Jesse was amazed of the size and unusual horn placement.

"No one does. They won't even come here to check it out for themselves."

"The falls must not have been here and this was just an open ended cave or   tunnel. They probably stayed here one winter and a cave-in blocked the entrances to the cave and they starved." Jesse's explanation for the fossilized animals was as scientific as possible given the evidence of the rock cave-ins. There were large skeletons as well as small ones. They all had horns. Jesse's explanation for the mass skeletal remains was a reasonable one.

(The remains were from the Soergel's Ox. Scientific name is *Soergelia mayfieldi.* This species of musk ox has been found throughout the United States as far south to Oklahoma and east to New York. They became extinct in the United States somewhere around 12-15 thousand years ago.)

"It sounds good to me," Alex had no explanation, so she accepted Jesse's explanation. After the exploration of the cave, they stayed a little longer to play in the pool. The sun was setting. It was time to get home before nightfall. Alex ran hand over Jesse's back and felt the scars.

"How did you get them?" She asked.

162

"I was about twelve when I got them," Alex didn't want to explain so he changed the subject.

"I think it's about time we got out and head for home," Jesse didn't want to talk about the scars, maybe someday he will reveal his past.

The sun was beginning to set, it was time to go home. They were feeling a bit frisky, so they ran the horses at full speed. After about twenty minutes, the horses were fully winded, so they stopped and walked them. They walked hand and hand and talked about everything. Jesse felt like he could tell her anything.

"Jesse, what kind of tree is this?"

"This is a female cedar. You can tell by the buds that cover the whole tree. The male cedar won't have buds," explained Jesse.

"When you are trying to clear cut cedars out of a pasture, you want to make sure that you get all the trees."

"Why?" Alex was a bit curious, since they had to clear new pasture land every spring to remove these trees.

"As it was explained to me, these evergreens are either male or female trees (dioecious) or having both the female and male tree in the same tree (monecious)."

The reason we clear cut is because of the fire danger in case of a prairie fire. They have oils in them that ignite the whole tree. The other reason is that they suck up water the grasses needed. Did you ever notice that grass doesn't grow where a cedar had been?"

Alex stopped and looked at Jesse, "I love the way you do this."

"Do what?" Asked Jesse.

"I love the way you explain things to me. You have so much information about nature in your head; it just spills out when you are outdoors. And, you are so good about sharing that information in a way that makes it so interesting. You are always teaching, whether it is with me or one of the men that works with you. How do you know so much about these things?" Alex asked.

She added, "You don't make me feel inferior because I don't already know. You just make sure I understand. You are a patient teacher and I love this about you. Maybe you should be a teacher."

"My parents made sure we went to school with

the nuns, who taught me. Father Juan Diego got me interested in the way nature works. He gave me the desire to learn."

Alex looked into Jesse's eyes. "You are like no other man I have ever known."

Jesse asked, "Is this good or bad?"

"Oh, definitely good," she said.

"You are such a hard worker. You give every ounce of strength and energy you have when you are cowboy. You are very tough guy when you need to be. Aunt Meg and Senor Sanchez talk about it all the time. They recognize what a good hand you are."

"And you are more of a gentleman than any man I know, always showing people respect. You are so good to me and treat me with such kindness. You make me feel special when I am with you. I have never known anyone like you, Jesse, and I feel so lucky that you like to spend time with me."

At one point Alex asked Jesse what it was like growing up in California. He said that it's like growing up here. She didn't want to press it, so she didn't ask any more about it. All she knew was that he was here, and that was all that mattered.

As they rode home, Jesse's thoughts were on their earlier conversations. What was the she trying to get out of him? She is so full of questions. How much do I let her in? The pain was still so raw. He knew he had to let go of it or it would burden his life and those around him. He'll tell her everything soon. He wanted no secrets between them.

{Nuestra Senora de la Merced-Our Lady of Mercy}

Juanita prayed that Jesse would find his way home. She was lonely without him, even though she had her family. Only a mother knows the pain of a missing child. This child was different. He had a special heart; he cared more about his family than he cared about himself. She didn't understand him, but she knew he was not home where he belonged. She prayed that no harm come to him and hoped he found what he was searching for. Jesse's brothers and sisters also missed him. They didn't understand why he had to go. They wanted him home.

From time to time Jesse sent a letter home to let them all know that he was fine. In his letters he described his adventures and mentioned each one by name so each would know that he was thinking about them. He mentioned that he missed them and someday he would return. It was not yet time to do so. He told them to count on each other and watch over their mother. At no time did he mention his dad. At the end of his letters he always wrote. I want you to pray for me. Pray for strength and courage. With the grace of God and Our Lady of Mercy's protection, I will return.

When Jesse left, Carlos, quit drinking. Everyone heard about what happened and why Jesse left. Carlos lost a lot of friendships over the incident. He lost the most from his own family. Carlos tried to mend things and was first to admit he had a problem with drinking. He became a regular church member and changed his attitude toward those who mattered, his family. He was kinder and give more of himself. It may have been too late for Jesse, but he wasn't too late for those who were still there. He regretted what had happened and hoped that Jesse would come home so he could explain and apologize for all that he had done. Carlos knew he had lost his son. Maybe his son would be the better man and forgive him.

{La Dia de Dios-this is God's Day}

Jesse wanted to go to Catholic Church but there wasn't one in town. Alex asked if he would accompany her to church along with Aunt Meg and Senor Sanchez. Jesse felt funny not going to mass, but a Baptist church was better than not going to church at all, and besides, it was another opportunity to be with Alex. Jesse didn't know the hymns as he pretended to sing them. He was not used to the whole way of worship. He decided just to watch and try to understand what was happening.

In his Church of Our Lady of Mercy, he was used to the rituals of the priest and the rhythm of the service. There was a familiar comfort that he knew every detail of the service. The nuns directed the children with the "clicker," as Jesse called it. Each click meant for the children to stand, sit, or kneel. He remembered that noise well from his youth. He was so well trained that to this day when he heard even the resemblance of a 'click', he was ready to stand, sit, or kneel.

There is one huge difference from the Baptist way and the Catholic way; the priest was the person who you spoke with to get to God. Baptist spoke to God directly. On the trail Jesse spoke to God directly, and he rather liked it that way. He would rather confess his sins to God than to another person. He would look further into this new church but, he still liked the Catholic Church's rich traditions.

Ever since he had asked God into his heart, he was different. His burdens were lighter and he knew he could always take them to the one who watches over him. His prayers were not always for him. He also prayed for those he loved. He prayed that all was well at home. He wanted to forgive but the wounds were still festering and he needed more time. He knew in order for God to forgive him, he must forgive those that caused him pain.

He was still new to this concept, but he was working on it. His prayers were for his family, his friends he left behind, new found friends and, of course, his special love, Alex.

After the service, they went home for Sunday lunch. Jesse liked the way the Lee's made the weekends so special. It seemed like a family, a happy family, and Jesse was a part of this family. He could stay and make this his home if they would let him. He didn't count on falling in love with Alex. He did not want to leave her. Maybe she could go with him to visit his friend Sam. He needed to get a letter to Sam to let him know where he was and his plans. He missed his friend. He would let him know where he was wintering. He so much wanted to let everyone know about Alex. Alex came by the bunkhouse to see if Jesse was ready to go on their walk. Jesse came to the door when she knocked.

"Ready?" She was happy to see him.

"Ready," he was just as happy to see her.

The two went hand-in-hand, carrying two cane

poles and bait to try their luck at fishing. They went to the widest pond in the area. The pond was surrounded by cattails, which made for good cover from the sun and prying eyes. The poles were ready and both went in ready to do their job. Alex laid out the blanket in the small clearing within the cattails for ground cover and another overhead for shade. Jesse was concerned about leaving the poles unattended, so he secured them to a cattail just in case they happened to catch something. Alex, on the other hand, just wanted to visit.

Jesse stood watching the poles, not really paying attention to Alex. She grabbed him from behind, and he fell flat onto his back. Alex jumped on top of him and they began to play fight. Jesse was so surprised that he reacted without thinking and flipped her to her back. He realized that he was being too rough with her, she was too small to be wrestling with her.

"Are you okay?" Jesse apologized and checked to see if he hurt her.

"I'm okay," it was her plan all along to get him to lie down next to her so they could talk.

"Jesse, I want to tell me more about your home, and your family."

Jesse told her about his brothers, sisters,

relatives, friends, and key people from his hometown. He even told of his experiences on the trail. Jesse told of everything she wanted to know, except for his father and what his life was really like. He wanted to hide his embarrassment and shame from being raised in an abusive home. Alex was perfect in his eyes. He didn't want her to think any less of him. He wanted her to see him, not his circumstances.

"I notice that you didn't say anything about your father," Alex was wanting to know more of his relationship with his father.

"There is not much to say about him. He had his way of doing, and I didn't agree with him."

"Are you anything like your father?" She thought it was so odd that a son would not mention anything about his father.

"No, I am not anything like my father. If anything I am totally opposite of him," Jesse said with a hint of irritation.

"Do you want me to stop asking you about him?"

"Yes, I would rather not talk about him. I'd rather talk about you and your parents." Jesse wanted to change the subject.

"Wait. What do you want to do with yourself? I

know that you don't want to help out here all your life."

"I want to go to the university and learn how I can produce a better wine. I need to understand about the grape plants themselves. How can we make a better plant so we can make a better wine? I want to have my own vineyard and have people come by to sample the wines."

"There are such schools in Madrid, but you know, I kind of like it here, and I wouldn't mind just staying here. I like what I see right here," Jesse was looking directly at her.

"Wait a minute. Are you telling me you would give up your dream just to stay here with me?" Alex was first happy to hear he wanted to stay, but she couldn't let him let go of his dreams for her.

"Dreams are dreams, and besides, I can be happy doing other things." Jesse was serious about changing his dreams. He had given his heart to her, and to give one dream up for the best dream, well, it was not even a choice. Jesse was being honest with Alex. Any man would give something up for the love of his life and would be content for the rest of his life for doing so. A man chooses his path and can live without regret. At this point, Jesse could not imagine life without Alex. He just didn't want to even think about it.

"Now, let's get back to my question. Tell me about your parents. Why did they let you come all this way to stay with your aunt? What do you want to do with yourself?" Jesse asked so she wouldn't ask questions.

"My parents are just too busy for me. They are so involved with their lives, and I was just in the way. That's how I see it, anyway. Aunt Meg has been like a mother, and most of the time she acts like it. I love her for it."

"How does Senor Sanchez fit in all this?" Jesse was looking for connections for everyone at the ranch.

"Aunt Meg, Uncle Tom, and Tony were the best of friends," Alex said.

"Who is Tony?" Jesse asked.

"Tony is what Aunt Meg calls Senor Sanchez when she thinks no one is around. I heard her call him that when she thought I was gone. His given name is Antonio, which translates to Anthony, which is shortened to Tony."

"I like him," Jesse felt that he wanted an honest relationship with him. He knew that he cared about Alex and him. Jesse decided it was time to confide in someone.

"What do you want to do with your life?" Jesse asked.

"I really don't know. I am supposed to start school here next fall. I really don't know."

"I wanted to help Aunt Meg run this place, but she tells me I must find something that I want for myself. She says a proper education is the thing to do for young ladies these days. I like ranching, but she says it is not the thing to do for this generation of women."

"What do you think?" She was looking for some sort of commitment from Jesse.

"I say you need to answer this one for yourself. I can't tell you what to do. It's your future, and you are the only one to answer that question," Jesse's answer was not the one Alex was looking for. She sighed and laid her head back on his chest.

She stopped questioning him about this family. She didn't understand why he would not answer her. She was thinking that he was not ready for a commitment yet. She wanted him to stay, but she loved him enough to let him go so he could fulfill his dream.

"Did you know my most favorite season is coming up?" Jesse looked up at the sky and noticed geese beginning to flock together and fly in their familiar V formation. They were readying them to fly to a southern location for the winter.

"What season is that?" Alex asked kissing Jesse on the cheek.

"I love the turning of the leaves, the colors of autumn, the smells of wood burning in the fireplace, the coolness of air when you wake. The smells of autumns Jesse turned on his side to get a better look at Alex.

"You are staying the entire winter, aren't you?" Alex was still trying to get Jesse to commit to stay longer.

"Yes, I am, and through part of the spring."

"Sanchez asked me to commit to bringing in the spring calves before I head off to Missouri."

"Can you just tell your friends to come out here to visit so we can meet them?" Alex didn't want him to leave.

"I suppose I can, but wouldn't it be better if one person went to them instead of four of them coming out to see one?" Jesse was thinking of the hardship on the family instead of him going east to see them.

"How about you come with me to Missouri so they can meet you?"

"Can I do that?" Alex excited about the possibility of going with Jesse.

"You'll have to ask your aunt to see if it is okay to do so."

"I can tell what the answer will be if I have to ask," Alex was pouting around like a little child who was told no.

"I guess that means I'll have to write you," Jesse, said getting a laugh at her expense.

"You're laughing at me and enjoying it, too?" Alex was now getting sore to how insensitive Jesse was toward the whole matter. So much so that she stood and walked away.

"Wait, I was only fooling around! I'm sorry about all of this, honest!" Jesse was not used to seeing someone cry on his account so he quickly went after her to see if she was okay.

"Hey, I'm sorry about that." Jesse went to comfort her and to make things better.

"How about I ask your aunt if you can go with

me to Missouri to visit friends? It is my idea, and I really do want you to come with me. This way, she will know that I really want you to come."

"Okay, but you are going to have to ask soon. I need to make sure that I can go. When the winter comes, everyone will have their minds on the cattle and the winter storms," being raised on the farm, Alex knew that winter preparations was all consuming.

"I think we were supposed to be fishing, and we haven't done any of that." Jesse was checked the lines and found bait taken.

"I caught what I wanted to catch," Alex said with a grin on her face.

"What?" Jesse didn't understand what she was talking about.

"Never mind, I have a better idea." Alex looked at Jesse's face, and when he caught her looking at him in that way, he knew exactly what was on her mind.

He didn't wait. He affixed the poles to the cattails and then invited her to lie down next to him with playful pat on the ground. Alex stood in the sun's light in front of Jesse, and the silhouette of her body was all he could see. Jesse looked at her and thought to himself how beautiful she really was and how lucky he was.

He held out his hand, and Alex took hold and then she went to her knees. Their eyes communicated their feelings and intentions. Alex made the first move and wrapped her arms around Jesse's neck. She whispered his name in a low, throaty tone, with the warmth of her breath in his ear.

And with that each tightening their grip around each other and then falling back. With Alex on his chest; they lay like that for several minutes not speaking. Alex raised her head and without a word still looking into his eyes she kissed him. Not the deep kiss that they have been accustomed to but a kiss that spoke of many things, a kiss so gentle that he wanted more but she left him wanting more. He understood this and still he wanted more and quickly turned her to her side. He returned the kiss and she responded. For the rest of the afternoon they were lost in each other. They lay there drifting in and out of a light sleep.

The sounds of the pond were much louder than usual. Song birds were singing their songs, grasshoppers sounding off, dragonflies and their much smaller cousins the damselflies skimmed the top of the water catching their prey. If you were still enough you could hear the sounds of wings fluttering. Bull frogs croaked and every now and again, a fish would breach the surface. From time to time, underbrush leaves would crackle beneath the hooves of a deer. The sounds of nature were everywhere.

Both still faced each other embraced. Alex used her finger to outline Jesse's face as if to memorize it. She closed her eyes for the briefest of moments and return with the look, a look of contentment. Jesse would mirror her and respond in kind. Each knew the others thoughts. A perfect fit. The closeness they now shared was what each wanted. They were as one; one in mind, one physically and one spiritually. A perfect fit.

With the afternoon almost gone, the two were still under the makeshift tent, not saying a word. They needed to get back. They gathered up their belongings and headed back to the ranch, happy that they had time to be alone together without interruption. Back at the ranch, they said their goodbyes, not wanting to, but knowing they had to attend to their responsibilities. Days went by, and everyone was getting the ranch ready for the upcoming winter. Much was needed to be done. Autumn was a time of preparation. With the days getting shorter, there wasn't much time for play.

{Winter Round up/Letter home}

Father Juan Diego
Our Lady of Mercy
San Joaquin Valley
Merced, California

November 10, 1890

Dear Padre Diego,

It has been sometime since I last wrote to you. All is well here with me. I have been fortunate to be taken in by the Lee family and am overwintering at the Lee's Ranch in the Valley of Still Waters, Oklahoma Territory.

I have had many experiences and met many memorable persons since I last wrote you. I hope this letter finds all of you well. You can write me here. I will be here through most of the coming spring. I plan to visit Sam in Missouri as soon as the spring storms have passed.

I pray my family is well. Tell them I miss them all and think of them often. I have stories to tell all from my adventures when I return.

Tell Sister Maria I have found what I have been looking for. The emotion is exactly what she described it would be. Her name is Alex. Finding her has changed me.

Padre, you were right, the one has protected me throughout my journey. I see things so differently from when I left that night. I even find that I can forgive my father. I won't forget what he did, but I can better understand him. I still do not want to see him; perhaps someday. I have missed you and our conversations.

Senor Antonio Sanchez, our ranch foreman, has befriended me, and I find that I am beginning to trust him. He tells me that his roots come from Waco, Texas. I think that is where my mom's family is from. Mrs. Lee is a caring lady. She watches over us boys as if she was our mom. Mrs. Lee is Alex's aunt. She runs the ranch for the US Calvary. I like her.

The boys are great. They work hard and find time to horse around when the work is done. George Washington Smith (GW), I find to be of good character and one of the toughest cowboys I have ever know, one that I would like to get to know better, I find him interesting. He always finds reason to smile.

In closing, I would like to say that I am becoming more of a man than I thought possible. To him I give all thanks.

Con Dios, Jesse

{Winter is here}

This was not a typical day. Sanchez got everyone up extra early. Sometime during the night, he had packed bags with several days of provisions. The boys were slow to get around. The bunk house was so cold that you could see your breath. Sanchez told everyone to get their warm clothes on and to bring their slicker riding coats and enough clothing for a few days.

"For a few days. Doesn't he know that it's cold out there?" TJ wondered what they could be doing that it would take a few days. And to think they would be out in the cold.

"Shut up, you girl. In fact you are worst than a girl," Cody had had enough of his crying.

"Why don't you just go put on a dress and get us out breakfast?" Cody continued his annoyance TJ's lack of mental toughness.

"I had enough of your lip. If you want to make something of it, then.....," TJ was getting his fill.

"Boys, enough! You will have plenty of time for that later. Get your stuff together. We have a whole lot of work to do this week. Go saddle up!" said Sanchez, who was tired of the nonsense himself. After a quick breakfast the headed out to the stable to pack. The boys were about to leave the stable when Alex rode up and blocked the entrance.

"Where are you going?" Jesse asked.

"The same place you are," Alex answered.

"Jesse, she comes with us. She has not missed this since she was 12," Sanchez said.

"Jesse, I can do anything you can, and maybe even better," she said in a teasing voice to diffuse the tension. Jesse was thinking to himself maybe so. If she was going to go with him to

Missouri, then he needed to see if she could handle the hard ride ahead. What better way to see if she could take the trail?

Sanchez explained what they were doing, and that it would take a few days to round up all the strays. They had to travel long distances to gather all of them and bring them back to the corrals. Many heads are lost every year to the storms, and some were taken by the Indians to eat.

Sanchez didn't think the cattle taken by the Indians were so much of a loss as they went to feed them. It was only right that the white man gave something back. What he didn't like was that many were stolen and given brands over the old ones. The stealing of cattle was punishable by imprisonment.

Sanchez didn't feel right about taking all the cattle back to the ranch. He had an understanding with the local Native Americans and let some of the cattle 'get away' from him. As far as he was concerned, they were the ones trespassing on Indian hunting lands.

The Oklahoma Territory and the unassigned lands made up the so-called Indian Territory of Oklahoma. When the Land Run of April 22, 1889, took place Indian land was taken. At high noon the run began and the unassigned lands were settled by whites. After the run, the Valley of the Still waters was the first settlement in the newly-opened lands to be settled.

The Santa Fe Railroad ran from north to south throughout the territory. Rail lines stretched from Arkansas City, Kansas to locations south. Stops along the way gave rise to towns overnight. Towns such as Guthrie were preplanned and laid out before the run actually occurred. In the morning of April 22, the town's population was zero. By nightfall, the town's population had grown to 10,000.

Many of the cattle stolen here were driven up to Kansas City and sold. Their job was to get as many as they could find before the first winter storms came. It was getting to be that time of the year. This is where the boys were to earn their keep for the winter.

A makeshift corral was built along the way to hold the cattle they found. TJ, GW, and Cody were left to guard them as the others rode on to find more strays. Orders were given that they were to stay with the cattle until they returned. A tent was erected to shield them from the north wind. TJ and Cody went out to search for cow wood (cow chips) to burn, and GW was left to get dinner started. Not much tree debris was to be found, so they gathered up the only fuel they could find, and that was cow wood. Dried cow dung burned hot and was easy to light. The two of them searched for hours to get enough to burn through the night. They knew their survival depended on the amount of fuel they found if a storm developed.

Sanchez, Jesse, and Alex kept to the cow trails and headed west to southwest in search of more strays. At sundown, they made camp. Their tent was erected, and the search for fuel to burn the camp fire began. With the necessary survival activities done, they stopped and began to get supper going.

It was a tiring day, not a lot was said. After the horses were cared for, they decided to call it a day. The tent was a two-man tent, but that was okay; they would sleep close to share the warmth of each other. With Alex in the middle, they settled in. Sanchez stayed up for a few hours, and the Jesses would take his turn guarding the campsite.

Each had the responsibility of making sure the fire did not go out. Their survival depended on it if the weather turned, and it kept the coyotes out of camp. Mainly it kept the two camps in sight of each other at least for the first night. Alex and Jesse welcomed this sleeping arrangement. They actually got to sleep for the first time with each other, even thought Sanchez was next to them. It didn't matter. They were side by side and knew what the other was thinking.

Jesse could feel the warmth of her body as he lay next to her, like two spoons in a drawer. Alex placed her hand on her top hip so Jesse could find it and they lay holding each other's hand and drifted off to sleep.

"Hey, Jesse it time." Sanchez gently nudged Jesse as so not to startle him awake. Sometime during the night, Sanchez had fixed a pot of coffee. Jesse welcomed the warmth from it. Alex stirred a little, but quickly settled into a new position and was asleep.

"She looks peaceful, doesn't she? Sanchez was pointing to Alex.

"She sure does," Jesse thought of how beautiful she was even in the dim light of the camp fire.

"Take good care of her," Sanchez said.

"I will," Jesse looked at Alex when he said it and thought what a responsibility it was to care for someone, not only to care for her physically, but to watch over her heart as well.

"I'm going to sleep." Sanchez tucked his blanket close across his neck and pulled his hat over his eyes.

Mariposa came over and begged for something to eat. Jesse gave her a bit of his hard biscuit, and she snorted and nudged him a little to show her approval. The night went without incident. Jesse stood guard and was grateful for the coffee. As the night wore on, his thoughts went from Alex to home. He wondered if things were any better. He prayed for them and then said one for the two he was watching over.

Jesse lightly, touched Senor Sanchez on the shoulder to let him know that it was his watch now. He made a new pot of coffee when he added more fuel to the fire. He settled in next to Alex in a sitting position with his revolver ready. Alex stirred a little. He held her hand until she was asleep again. Jesse thought to himself how lucky he was to have met this family.

"Hey, Cody," TJ had been rolling over in his bedroll for most of the night.

"What?" Cody was trying to sleep and was irritable.

"Do you suppose there are Indians out there?"

"Let's see, this is Indian Territory-Oklahoma. What do you think?"

"I was just asking," TJ was wanting to have a bit of conversation since he couldn't sleep.

"Sorry, I've been on edge this whole day. I am tired, cold and hungry," Cody said in an apology to TJ.

"I'm a little cold myself," TJ said.

"We'll earn our keep this week," TJ was thinking back to when he was hired, and Mrs. Lee said that this day would happen.

"I hope the weather holds out. This time of the year, you never know when a storm might come down from the north," TJ looked at the sky and noticed that it was a cloudless night.

"It'll be your watch in an hour. You better get some shut eye," Cody added more cow wood to the fire and started a new pot of coffee going. He could see Sanchez's fire off in the distance.

"I'll take the next watch," GW said.

"Okay, I'll wake you in about 4 hours," Cody added more cow wood and started a new pot of coffee.

The night was without incident for both camps until first light. Sanchez was wakened by the sounds of horses riding close to camp. At first light, Sanchez woke Jesse up. A hunting band of Osage stopped a distance from the camp.

"Hey saddle up and come with me. Don't wake Alex." Sanchez was motioning Jesse to keep quiet.

Jesse exited the tent and was stretching when he noticed the visitors. Without thinking, he reached for his revolver. Sanchez stopped him with a finger over his mouth to let Jesse know to keep quiet.

"It's okay. They're Osage. We are going out to meet them. They won't come into the camp."

"What do they want?" Jesse still wanted to pull out his revolver.

"They are here for a few head of cattle to feed themselves during the winter." Sanchez said.

After they were saddled they rode out to acknowledge them. Greetings were exchanged along with introductions. Jesse was new to them. Jesse found them to be friendly. He wanted to know more about them. After they received their cows, the leader of the band invited them to their village. It was agreed that Jesse would visit them after they got back to the ranch.

"Why do you want to see their village?" Sanchez asked Jesse.

"Curiosity, I suppose," said Jesse.

"I've met many tribes along the way from California and have found them to be quite friendly."

"Well, let's get back to work and get these strays home. I don't want to get caught out here when the weather changes." Sanchez looked up at the morning sky, trying to get a fix as to what the weather would be like this day.

Arriving back at camp they found Alex irritated, "That wasn't nice of you to just leave me here."

"Thought it was best for you to watch camp," said Sanchez.

"You could have awakened me to watch camp," Alex was still annoyed with the both of them.

"I saw you with those Indians. Are they the same ones that you always give cows to?" Alex asked Sanchez.

"They are different ones," Sanchez replied.

"Are they friendly?" asked Alex.

"Yes. They are Osage," said Sanchez.

"Good to know, are we breaking camp?" asked Alex.

"After breakfast," replied Sanchez.

The next couple of days it was work as usual. They picked up about 50 head and a dozen mustangs. It was time to get them back to the ranch and settle in for the winter. Much remained to be done before winter hit. The ranch was waiting for the winter feed from the Army for horses and cattle. Late November was not a time to rest. Remounts needed to be broken and cattle needed to be cared for. There was always something to do on a ranch before they could call it a winter. The last of the vegetables had to be canned.

{Dinner at the big house}
Telephones were still in their infancy in the territory. Communications was either by overland mail through the stage, rail service, or by telegraph. Mail to the ranch usually came in with the stage or by Cavalry courier. A telegraph messenger delivered a telegraph to Meg.

Greetings, Margaret. We will arrive Saturday on the 3pm train from Kansas City...Stop... We will stay for a week...stop...We have a surprise for Alexandria...stop... Hope all is well...Joseph... Stop.

Coming in from four days of rounding strays,

they were dog-tired and just wanted to take hot baths, change into clean clothes, get a hot meal and sleep on something soft. They had a few hours before that could happen. Strays had to be put up and the livestock had to be properly tended to.

"All of you come to the big house when you're through for supper," announced Meg.

They smelled the stew, biscuits and the apple pies as they came into the ranch. There is nothing like eating well after a job well done, not to mention sleeping on a full stomach with decent food instead of trail provisions. With everything taken care of, they gathered for fellowship and a well-deserved meal. Everyone was on their best behavior as they were in Mrs. Lees' home instead of eating in the bunk house. It was a treat to be in the big house. It gave the boys a sense of being a part of a family. As the boys walked in, they saw a table set with china, glassware and silver, all laid out as if it were a Thanksgiving dinner.

As the boys caught sight of Mrs. Lee and Alex coming down the stairs with their evening dresses on they stood without being told to. Usually the women didn't wear such fancy dresses on the ranch. Tonight was a special occasion. Meg was happy that things on the ranch were going well and thankful that the young men were hard working and got along with each other. She always grew fond of them. They were her children while on the ranch. The boys waited until Mrs. Lee and Alex were seated before they sat themselves.

"Alex, can you say the blessing tonight?" Meg asked Alex as she was seated.

"Remove your hats and bow your heads," said Alex, who prayed.

"Dear Lord, we come to you with thanksgiving in our hearts for watching over us as we went to recover lost ones and brought them back home. We want to honor you by our prayers and actions as we try to do our best in your eyes. Thank you for bringing us new friends to share in fellowship. Thank you, Lord, for providing for us in all things and blessing us in ways that we may not know. Bless this meal and those that prepared it. These things I say in your name. Amen."

They all said, "Amen."

"Eat as much as your stomachs can hold. You all deserve it. Tomorrow is Friday, and I think we can sleep in for a bit before we get to work. You all deserve a good night's sleep." Meg raised her glass and offered a toast to all of them.

"Yes ma'am. We surely appreciate the time to rest up and get the trail out of us," TJ said.

Everyone was in good spirits and brought home a story to share. Jesse was thankful their adventure ended well.

"Alex, I am going to visit the Osage village in the next few days, so I won't be around. I wanted to get to know them. I met a few Pawnee before I arrived in town. It's good to get to know the tribes in the area. You never know when we can help each other," Jesse said.

"Oh, I almost forgot. Can I have time off to visit them?" Jesse forgot to ask permission before he announced his plans.

"It appears like everything is almost caught up with around here," Meg glanced over at Tony to see if he approved.

"It would be safer if you took someone with you," Sanchez looked at Jesse to make sure he understood that that's the only way he could go.

"Yes sir, but I have visited other tribes along my way here and have always gotten along with them."

"Can I come?" Alex was so hoping that he would

invite her.

"You better ask your aunt first," said Jesse.

"Why is it that I always have to ask permission? I'm just as old as you are, Jesse!" Alex took offense at his answer. Meg decided this was the right time to bring up the new of the telegraph.

"Oh, Alex, I almost forgot. I have a surprise for you. I received a telegraph today. Your parents will be coming on the 3pm train from Kansas City on Saturday."

"What? Why?" Alex obviously was taken aback by the news, and Jesse was thankful for the diversion.

Alex looked at Jesse with a look that worried him. Her face was not one that was thrilled to have her parents come visit. He decided he would not mention it at all unless she said something about it. It was getting late. Everyone thanked Aunt Meg for her hospitality and for the extra time to sleep in the next morning. Having a full stomach and good company would make their sleep more restful. Each took a refill of coffee and made his way to the bunk house.

Tony and Meg stayed in the dining room to talk about the upcoming visitors. Family was coming, and they had to get things ready for them. They each had a concern about how Alex took the news.

Lagging behind, Jesse stayed on the porch, hoping that Alex would want to talk about her parents. She had the look of someone trying to figure things out. He asked her if she wanted to visit. She politely said that she was tired and needed to rest. It was obvious she had a lot on her mind.

He went to the stables where he put Mariposa in for the night. He made sure she had plenty of fresh water and grain for the night. Her winter blanket came in while they were out. He placed it on her, and she let him know that it was strange putting a blanket on her.

"Hey there I know you don't like this, but you need your rest, too. I'll let you out early in the morning," Jesse gently stroked her neck with a brush.

"I hope her parents approve of me. Well, I guess I'll find out. Good night, girl,"
As he was leaving the stables he looked over to Alex's room. The light had just went out.

"Good night, Alex," He stayed looking at the window just in case she decided to stay up. Maybe she would come out and visit with him.

He stayed in the stable for over an hour waiting for Alex. She didn't come. He finally decided that it was not going to happen. Getting into bed, he prayed as he always did. It was going to be a restless sleep. His mind was on Alex, her parents, his family, and what he was going to in the spring. Having trouble sleeping, he dressed and made his way to the stable. He began to work, thinking that he needed to work this out before he could sleep. Sanchez watched him leave the bunkhouse. He was the last to sleep and the first one to wake. This was going to be a difficult night for him, also.

{And the truth shall set you free}
"Hey wake up!" said Cody, tapping Jesse's shoulder.

"Enough!" With outstretched arms reaching to fight off his dream, Jesse woke from a nightmare.

"You must have been having a bad one," said Cody

"Hey it must have been a really bad one. You were trying to fight someone in your sleep. You kept saying you're never treating me this way again over and over," Cody was just out of arm reach.

"Yea, some of it was in Mexican, too," TJ added.

"It's called Spanish, you idiot," said Cody

"What does no ma, termina esta noche mean?" TJ asked.

"It means no more, it ends tonight," GW answered for Jesse.

"You understand Spanish?" Jesse asked GW.

"I know some," GW said.

"Don't you boys have something to do?" asked Sanchez.

"Yes, sir, we were just trying to.....," Cody was cut short when Sanchez looked at him. The look said, "No more excuses."

"Okay, we've going," Cody decided it was best to leave it alone and get to work.

"Jesse, maybe it's time we talked about what really brought you here," Sanchez placed a hand on Jesse's shoulder.

"Okay, can it wait until later today? I need to talk with Alex this morning. I promise I will talk to you about this," Jesse was obviously not wanting to visit with Senor Sanchez.

"Okay, you know where to find me. There's not much we're doing today. We'll handle things here. I expect to see you this afternoon. We need to go to town, you and me," Sanchez was waiting for this since Jesse arrived. There was something so familiar about him. He just couldn't figure out what it was.

"Jesse, if you want to talk..," GW gave Jesse that all too familiar smile. Meg told Jesse that she last saw Alex heading to the stables. Jesse knew exactly where she would go when she needed to be alone. He saddled Mariposa.

What would make her so upset about her parents coming to visit? Is she upset with me for wanting to go to the Osage village when her parents are coming or was is it because I said she had to ask permission to accompany me?

Whenever Alex had something to hash out, she headed to Brush Creek Falls. This was one place where she found solitude. Sam was kept to an easy deliberate pace. Alex took in the change of season. She loved this time of the year. Everything about the change in season gave her the sensation of what was right in the world. The season brought the warmth of a fire to sit and read by. The vivid colors of the leaves right before they fell were at their most colorful. It was a time of thanksgiving for the work they put in during the year.

The ranch almost could almost run itself during the winter. The daily chores were milking the cows, feeding livestock and making sure there were enough Army horses were ready to be shipped out. The winter brought fellowship where everyone came together to play games and to tell stories. It was a time of Thanksgiving. It was also a sad time. The deep winter brought death. Suffering always accompanied winter. The season weeded out the weak, which is nature's way. The weeding out of less desirable people was not nature's way but man's way. It is man's way no matter what the season.

Now that she had someone special to share it with, this season would be memorable. She was thankful for his coming. He made her happy, and now she had to think about her parents and how to make them see how things were between Jesse and her. She circled the area to make sure critters were not hiding in the leaf litter. She dismounted and laid out a blanket. She paused and took in the season before she set her mind on what to say to her parents.

The sun's rays shone through spots in the canopy, which added warmth to the shade. Water over the falls was almost to a trickle. The late autumn rains which feed them were late. The cattails, now dormant showed top of the underwater entrance to the cave. Since the rains were late, the pool was shallower. Leaves floated on the surface. The edges of the pool had a thin layer of ice.

"Maybe this is going to be a light winter," Alex said to Sam.

"How am I going to explain Jesse to my parents?" She thought. "They don't understand how thoughtful he is or how he cares for me."

The sounds of the wooded area were heard as soon as she stopped talking to Sam. Several deer with their yearlings slowly walk to the pond. The last of the insects busied themselves with perpetuating the species. Soon their life cycle would be over. The cycle of life continues.

Winter plumages of overwintering birds were in full color. Other birds were making preparations to migrate to winter home ranges. Constant chattering of squirrels was everywhere. The rush for this year's acorn harvest was on. Animals everywhere were getting their winter coats. Everywhere you looked, animals were either getting food storage prepared or finding enough food to add to their fat storage. The most fit would help ensure their survival until spring. That was nature's way.

"They will see him as hired help, a cowboy with

nothing on his head but a hat," Alex said out loud to Sam.

"They won't even take the time to really get to know him. They don't know him like I know him. He wants more out of life than drifting from ranch to ranch. He wants to make something of himself."

Jesse urged Mariposa to pick up the speed; he was anxious to get to Brush Creek. He didn't take the time to notice the change of seasons, his mind was on Alex. Upon arriving he dismounted even before Mariposa came to a halt.

"Hey, I am sorry that I upset you. I don't have to go the village right away. I can wait until your parents leave," Jesse didn't give Alex a chance to say a word.

"Really, I can wait, and I am sorry that I made you feel like you were a child in front of everyone. I thought since you were living at your aunt's ranch, she was responsible for you, and I didn't want her upset with me."

"No, no, that's not it, Jesse," Alex put her hand over his mouth to stop his talking, and then kissed his face.

"You didn't upset me. I was thinking about how

my parents, well, how they are going to see you."

"What do you mean, how are they going to see me?" Jesse was getting upset instead of hearing what she had to say.

"I'm afraid they won't see the real you as I see you," Alex was trying not to hurt his feeling.

"I don't understand; how would they see me?" Jesse was noticeably upset.

"They will see only what they want to see," Alex was trying to explain her parents.

"I see you as an intelligent, hardworking, determined and compassionate person. You are like no other I ever met, person who knows who he is and what he wants to be."

"What are you trying to say, Alex?"

"This may hurt you, but they want someone of substance to be with me. They will only see that you are hired cowboy and the color of your skin."

"They don't even know me. How can they judge me because I work on a ranch? And to judge someone because of the color of their skin is just wrong."

"I'm not like them. I love you because I know you. I want to be with you. I have never been so happy," Alex said as she hugged him.

"I want you to go to the Osage on Friday. I want a day with them to get them used to the idea of us."

"An individual should be judged by his character, not the color of one's skin," Jesse said. He took several deep breaths and settled himself. He needed to be in control of his emotions before he said something that he would regret later.

They spent the morning discussing her parents. This led to Alex wanting to have answers about his family. He had been avoiding answering these questions since they met. It was only right that he answered her questions now, yet he was afraid that he might be judged for his past. Jesse had given his heart to her. He had total faith in her, and so he told of his life. For the first time, his most secretive thoughts were out in the open. Alex listened to him without interruption. As he talked he kept his head down and avoided looking at her. He was waiting for some response from her. He didn't know what to expect from her.

As the afternoon sun broke through the morning fog, he finally was to a point where he needed to hear from her that it was okay. What he got was someone with tears in her eyes and a hug that enveloped his soul. He knew then that it was going to be all right. As they rode back he continued to talk about his travels. From time to time he paused to think about how he should disclose the details of some events; he knew that he had to be completely open with her. He continued to tell of himself until the ranch was in sight.

He felt a closeness he had never had, a trust that he had never felt. He could tell things to Sam, Lee, and even to Padre Diego, but to tell Alex was different. The burden of hiding things was lifted; he was free of his past. As they got closer to the ranch, Alex asked Jesse if he would take someone with him to Osage encampment. He told her that he would. He didn't want anyone to worry about him. His ranch family need not worry about his safety. She pointed out that the ranch family would worry if he didn't take someone with him. They were connected, and family worries about the safety of all. He said he would ask GW if he could accompany him. Alex slid Sam closer to Mariposa and held out her hand. Jesse held it for a bit, and right before he let her go, he gently squeezed it.

"Thank you for sharing this with me," Alex said. I know it must have been difficult for you to tell. With all that you have been through, you didn't let it change you."

"We make a choice to hate or to love. Life is about making choices. We don't let our circumstances define who we are. My circumstance made me a better person. I have to go see someone now," Jesse said to Alex as she dismounted.

"Who is that?" she asked.

"Senor Sanchez. I need to visit with him."

"When will you leave, and how long will you leave?" Alex was concerned about Jesse's welfare.

"First light tomorrow I plan on being gone not more than the weekend."

"Hey Jesse, I love you."

"I love you too, Alex," with a tip of his hat and a smile on his face, Jesse went to meet with Senor Sanchez, who was at the barn visiting with Meg. He led Mariposa and Sam to the corral, took off their gear, and turned them loose.

"Here he comes; hope you get something out of him," Meg said with her fingers crossed.

"Are you ready to visit?" Sanchez gave that head nod that men understand.

"Yes sir," Jesse gave the same nod back. Tipping their hats to Meg, they left for town.

"Get everything talked out with Alex?" Sanchez asked as soon as they cleared the big house.

"Yes sir," Jesse answered him turning his head to Sanchez.

"She thinks that it would be better if I visited the Osage when her parents first arrive. She tells me they won't approve of me."

"What do you think about that?" Sanchez asked.

"I'm upset about how they might look at things. I'll do as she asks. I guess I'd feel different if my daughter brought home someone for me to meet."

"Just be yourself, which is all you can do. Give them time to see how happy Alex is."

"I'm afraid they will convince her that I am not right for her and make her give me the mitten." Jesse looked straight ahead, not making eye contact with Sanchez.

"Wait a minute. What I do know is that she really cares about you, and she is about as stubborn as a mule. I think she knows her mind, and nobody is going to convince her about nothing." Sanchez bumped Jesse's shoulder with his own to get his attention.

"You're right," Jesse shrugged his shoulders.

"How about we stop up here and visit some? I think it's time we talk about things," Sanchez slowed the wagon and stopped short of the road that led into town.

"Yes sir," Jesse understood what he wanted.

They spent the better part of the afternoon talking about Jesse's journey to Oklahoma. Sanchez mostly listened. Every now and again Jesse would ask Sanchez for his thoughts. Their conversation was one that a father and son would have. They laughed at some things and were serious at others. All the while, they respected the words spoken.

Jesse needed a man's perspective and guidance on questions he had. His own father would not have engaged in such conversations. Jesse had those delicate questions that only an older more experienced man would know the answers to. He sought the advice of someone who cared and valued women. And so it was, they openly spoke from their hearts, and judgment was not on their minds.

"Did you remember to get those ingredients I needed?" Meg called to them as they parked the wagon in front of the house.

"I just had to tell them who it was for, and they had it in the wagon before I left," Sanchez said with a wink and grin.

"Jesse takes the wagon to the barn, get the rest of the supplies off, and then go find the boys and tell them to call it a day."

"Yes sir." Jesse gave a slight nod that said thanks for everything.

When he was out of sight, Meg asked Sanchez if he found out anything. Knowing that things were said in confidence, he didn't want to sever the trust. He told her that Jesse was a young man who wanted to make it on his own. He told of his family and what his dreams were. Some of the dark past experiences were left out. Sanchez felt Jesse's pain. He couldn't understand how Jesse kept the dark heart from coming out. Jesse was looking for approval.

What Jesse lacked in social experience he more than made up for in how he respected others. Without the encouragement of a father, he still had self- confidence and self-assurance, and basically, he liked himself. His demeanor was one of self-reliance or self-sufficiency and not one of arrogance or conceit.

"I think the boy is on the right path. He certainly has more life experiences than his age indicates," Sanchez said.

"I like him," Meg said.

"He is a determined young man, that's for sure," Meg added.

"Alex sure likes him. I see the way they look at each other," Tony added.

"What do you think, Tony?" Megan needed his opinion on the kids' relationship.

"I think we should just leave them alone," Tony patted Megan's hand.

"I think you are right. She has a mind of her own, and besides, she is as stubborn as it gets, and like someone I know," Megan looked in Tony's direction.

"Say, do you have any of that pecan pie left?' Tony asked.

"I think I have a slice or two left over, but isn't it a bit early for pie?"

"It's never too early or too late for a piece of

your pie," Tony placed a hand on the small of her back and they entered the house.

{Osage village}
The next morning, GW and Jesse were dressed before the sun was up. Senior Sanchez was still in the rack, so they started the first coffee of the day. They intended to go to the village right after they looked for strays. The chilly morning was a two-cup morning. Work waited for them, and it was getting too cozy in the bunk house sipping coffee.

They had gotten the okay to go but felt they still had to do some work before leaving the ranch. They were paid to work. Senor Sanchez and the boys had worked it out and were given the task the night before. The moon was still hanging high when they mounted the horses. They were conscious of their obligations to the ranch. Two hours later, strays they found were in the pens. It was time to get another cup of coffee and some breakfast. The rest of the crew was sitting down to breakfast. It was a quiet morning. They joined them for a bite and refill of coffee; then it was off to the village.

"Make sure you announce yourselves before you enter the village. Do not enter the camp until you get the okay to do so. Dismount slowly and walked the horses in," Sanchez said as last minute directions to the boys.

"Did you remember to get a gift for the chief?" Sanchez was making sure they had not forgotten. It was proper ritual to bring a gift.

"Yes, I think this bowie knife will do," GW said.

"You two be careful, and remember where and who you are. I expect you to be home by the weekend. Don't make me look for you, and above all, do not interfere. You are guests," Sanchez gave each his customary handshake and sent them on their way.

Sanchez has had a good relationship with the Osages ever since the ranch was put into operation. He found them to be peaceful enough. Cattle, medicine, and other provisions were given, and in exchange, they were allowed to pick up strays on the hunting grounds. He had found Principle Chief James Bigheart to be a man of peace who wanted his people to survive with the White man. He was still hesitant about letting the boys go. He knew that Jesse had to go to satisfy his curiosity. In his youth, he would have done the same.

"Hey, thanks for riding with me, GW," Jesse was grateful for his companionship.

Ever since he left the San Joaquin, he has had a fascination with the Native Americans. Most of the Native Americans he encountered were sociable, accommodating, and inquisitive. Others were apprehensive of strangers, rightfully so.

"No problem. Why do you want to do this?" GW asked.

"I just wanted to know more about them. Ever since they came into my camp, I was curious about them."

"Well, your curiosity just might get you killed someday. I know a little something about them," GW's tone changed to a more somber one.

"Okay, tell me about them," GW got Jesse's attention.

"They are not as friendly as you might think. They have many enemies, especially amongst the other tribes. My grandmother and father told stories of how they treated their captives. There was this one battle known as The Cutthroat Gap Massacre," GW made a throat-slashing movement.

"What does that mean?" Jesse asked.

"That means that the heads of their captives were cut off and placed on pots so all could see," GW again made the throat-slashing sign.

"I've heard many tales how the tribes treated captives. It was pretty gruesome stuff," GW added.

"Do you think that is pretty much like all warring tribes? We can't say much about the so-called civilized Americans. Look how we treated each other during the Civil War. Look how we treat the Indians today. I don't see any difference between us and them," Jesse pointed out.

"You are right about that," GW said in agreement.

"Look what happened to you the other day in the saloon, just because of the color of your skin. It's just not right," Jesse shook his head in disgust.

"Being right has nothing to do with it. It has been that way with man since the beginning. Try being me," GW pointed out his heritage and the prejudice he had to endure. His ancestors were slaves brought over from the African continent. After escaping from a Georgia plantation, his grandparents were captured by the Cherokee (the name Cherokee is a Creek Indian word, the name for the tribe in the Cherokee language is Tsalagi or Aniyunwiya) and enslaved again.

The "Nunna Daul Isunyi," the trail where they cried, was when the United States Government and the state of Georgia forced relocation of 15,000 Cherokees to the Indian and Oklahoma territory, not counting the nations of the Chickasaws, Creeks, Seminole, and the Choctaw. Each nation has its own trail of tear story to tell. The ethnic cleansing of the Native Americans from the eastern United States, and especially Georgia, was executed by the signing of the Indian Removal Act of 1830 by President Andrew Jackson. The signing of the Act was hastened due to finding gold on the Cherokee lands by illegal prospectors.

Of the almost 15,000 Cherokee, more than 4,000 died due to winter conditions and disease. On this death march, his grandmother's man died. GW didn't know if he was her husband. At the time, she was very young. Upon settling into the Oklahoma Territory, his grandmother was raped. His mother was the result of that act. His mother's husband was Cherokee.

Years after arriving in the territory, the Cherokee slaves were freed. Former black slaves became members of the tribe while others chose to leave and establish their own towns in the territory. The Native American Indian slaves were freed to return to their own tribes or stay with the tribe as members.

White men came to marry the Cherokee women so that they could get government Indian land because of the Indian head rights. Only after many unsolved deaths of Indian wives did the government and the Cherokee outlaw the marriages.

"I like this country. It tolerates men like me. I'll head west as the country gets more civilized," With his familiar grin, GW told of his intentions in the spring.

"What do you mean, men like you?" Jesse asked.

"You know, of mixed blood," GW said.

"Oh?" Jesse was taken off guard from his remark.

"As I see it, we are all the same," Jesse said.

"You need to open your eyes, partner. Some people tolerate better than others. I, for one, prefer open country with fewer people. Jess, you're from out the way. How are things out West?"

"Well, it depends. I suppose acceptance is given to those who don't have something they want. The Chinese are tolerated because they work on the railroad. Native Americans are not.

Hispanics are, only if they stay out of the way. I just don't understand it all."

"You are a ways from home my friend," GW said with an uplifted eyebrow.

"Yep, I left to find out some things on my own," Jesse answered.

"Found them?" GW asked.

"Getting there," Jesse answered with a smile.

"I think you have found something in Miss Alex," GW again lifting the eyebrow and this time with a smile.

"I found one of them with her, others through my travels and still searching for other things from myself."

"I think we all go through life searching for one thing or another," answered GW.

"Take happiness. Some search all their lives and never find it, while others find it right off," GW the philosopher said.

"Tia Silvia told me, happiness is not perfected unless it is shared. I think she is right." Jess smiled as he saw her in his mind.

"Shared joy is double joy. Shared sorrow is half sorrow. This is what my mama told me," GW said.

"Your Mama was a wise one," Jesse added.

The Osage encampment was a day and half ride north and east of the Valley of the Still Waters. They spoke of their families and of plans after the spring. Jesse found it easy to talk to GW. Telling Alex and Sanchez made opening up to GW much easier.

Both had stories to tell, and each was looking for someone to entrust their stories to. It is not an easy thing for a man to trust another man with his story. When there is trust, men will usually say things in a straightforward way without hidden meaning.

"I guess this makes us saddle partners, you recon?" GW asked.

"I guess you're right. Well partner, it feels good to have a partner," Jesse leaned over offering his hand to GW.

"Yes, it does," They shook hands on it and that's all it took. Each had the others back.

They reached the encampment in late afternoon. They stopped and waited until someone spotted them. They made no sudden movements that sentries could interpret as hostile. They made their presence known and made their way to meet Principal Chief James Bigheart. All eyes were on the two outsiders. As they were lead to the center of the village, both took notice of three Indian captives tied to posts in middle of the village. Children were harassing them with sticks and stones. Some were using pointless arrows, shooting at them for target practice. They were a ways from them and surrounded by Osage, so Jesse could not make them out.

"How tall are they," asked Jesse referring to the Osage.

"I say about 6' to 7', I say," GW said.

"Keep your hands up away from your body," Jesse reminded GW.

"I know, I know. Remember who you're talking too," GW said.

They were met by an individual who came into the round up camp. Jesse recognized him. Greetings were exchanged outside the Principal Chief's lodge through an interpreter. The interpreter was a young girl Jesse thought to be about 16 years old. She was Cherokee in appearance, but her dress was that of an Osage woman, no doubt captured at a young age, GW pointed out. She spoke both Osage and Cherokee.

The girl spoke first. The language used was Cherokee, an Iroquoian language, and the Osage, a Siouan language. GW translated the Cherokee. Her Cherokee was difficult to understand, but enough was understood to make out what she said.

"It is good that you came to visit. Welcome," she said.

"I am happy to be here," Jesse answered and nodded his head to show them that he was happy to be there.

"Come inside. Chief Bigheart is waiting to meet you," she said.

The lead warrior, the interpreter, GW and Jesse went into the lodge. They stood until the Chief motioned them to sit. The lodge floor was covered with buffalo hide. A small fire hearth was in the middle of the lodge with an opening that let the smoke out. It was comfortable surroundings. The Chief spoke first, as was customary.

"I was told that you might come to visit us someday. It is a rare meeting when someone comes in peace. The Blue Coats want this land.

Other tribes want our horses, our food, our land, and our blood." Chief Bigheart said through the interpreter,

"Chief Bigheart, I come because I am curious about your people. Throughout my travels I have encountered many tribes and clans. I have learned much from each," Jesse said. The interpreter translated the words.

"This is good that we should meet to know one another. Knowledge brings understanding, and that brings peace. Your Sanchez is a man of peace and honor. If he sends you this way you also must be men of peace," Chief Bigheart placed his hand over his heart to indicate this.

They exchanged pleasantries, and then GW gave the Chief the Bowie knife. The gift signified that they came in friendship. The Chief gave GW a long bow and a quiver of arrows made from the Bodark tree. The tree is also known as the Osage orange. The wood of the Bodark does not decay easily. The Long Bow of the Osage Indians were renowned for its strength and craftsmanship.

After the exchange of gifts, they were led outside to walk the village. Jesse's curiosity overcame him, and he asked why those men were tied to posts. He knew that he was told not to interfere, but he just could not leave this alone. The Chief said that they were captured when they failed to get away with several ponies. They are to be executed for what they did. It had been this way since time began.

"Would it be better to let them go and send them a message that it is better to live in peace? It would be a sign of friendship to let them go?" Jesse asked.

"Hey, leave this alone. You know what Sanchez said. We are guests in the village. Maybe you should count how many Osage and how many of us. By my count, we are a few shy of being even," GW said, while smiling not to let their host see that they were not trying anything.

"I think I know them; they are the ones who came into my camp before I was hired on, I think," Jesse said.

"What?" GW didn't know any of this.

"This is no time to thinking," GW said in a hushed voice.

"They came into my camp and were looting my saddle bags, and one was trying to rope my horse. We ended up sitting down, exchanging gifts and parted friends. I can't let this go." Jesse was adamant about getting them released.

"Are you sure?" GW was questioning the wisdom of Jesse's actions.

Jesse took a better look, "Yes, I recognize them."

"You know that could be us. You would want your friends to come help." Jesse said.

"It could be us sooner than you think. A Mexican and a black Cherokee inside of an Osage camp and you are defending the lives of a Pawnee scout party!" GW smile vanished.

"I for one would like my stuff not to be sliced open if you don't mind," GW looked down at his crotch.

"Chief Bigheart, I know these warriors. They too came into my camp to steal my horse. We sat down as warriors and talked about how to resolve our differences. We met as enemies and left as men of peace," Jesse said.

"Chief Bigheart is it better to have counsel with our enemies and find understanding, and with that understanding, bring peace," Jesse brought his word back to him.

"I see that you were listening to my words," Chief Bigheart said.

"Will you fight for them?" Chief Bigheart asked.

"Would you risk your lives for them knowing that you would certainly be killed for your efforts?" Chief Bigheart pointed to each of them.

Jesse started this and now had to find the words to make clear that he would do the same for the Osage. He was risking not only his life but that of GW as well, maybe Senor Sanchez was right. He shouldn't have interfered.

"I would fight for my Native American friends if it calls for it. I defend the lives of my Pawnee brothers as I would fight for my Osage brothers. Are we not men of peace?" Jesse slowly unbuckled his gun belt and held it above his head, and then placed it on the ground in front of the Chief. Jesse motioned for GW to do the same.

"I ask you to think about releasing them to us and show your willingness for peace amongst the Pawnee, great Chief Bigheart," Jesse opened his arms wide and then crossed them across his chest in the form of an X to signify a sign of peace

"Let us counsel on this. You are young, but you have said things that are true," The Chief called for a council of Elders.

The Chief and others went inside to discuss the

situation. GW and Jesse were free to roam the village. Jesse asked that the Pawnee captives be left alone until after the counsel. The word was given; the Pawnees were given water and left alone, at least for the time being.

Jesse and GW went to the Pawnee, cared for their wounds, and watched for their safety. The wounds indicated that they had been captives for some time. Their faces were beaten and swollen, with deep lacerations on their chests. Some of the cuts still bled. Other cuts were closed with dried blood. They couldn't tell which was blood or red paint. GW took water and washed off everything.

"Hey, this could be us, you know," GW said as he washed off the blood.

"I know I couldn't just stand by and watch this," Jesse answered.

"We can't stop this. It has been going on like this since the beginning. It is their way," GW said.

"I have to try," Jesse couldn't stand anyone to suffer.

The warrior's scalp locks were cut off to signify disgrace that they had been captured, the uttermost humiliation. Each was stripped of their loin cloths with their penis cut lengthwise just deep enough to bleed with string tied to their testes so children can pull on them. Countless puncture wounds made by pointless arrows were found on their bodies.

Once Jesse knew the Pawnees were cared for, he surveyed the camp. The village went back to daily life. Every once in a while someone looked their way. Preparations for the upcoming winter were the main task at hand. He knew that his scene was played out for incalculable generations amongst countless tribes. What right did he have to interfere with what had been done since time began? The Osage had been at war with the Pawnee long before they came to the Oklahoma Territory. They were doing what they had always done, protecting property and loved ones. The interpreter and GW were off walking the village. He stayed behind to continue the first aid care for them. This scene could have been at the Pawnee village. He would have done the same. Why do men do such things?

"What is your name?" GW finally asked her.

"Niabi," she replied, looking up at GW.

"What does it mean?" GW understood bits of the Osage language.

"It means Fawn," she said.

"What is your Cherokee name?" he asked.

"How did you know that I am Cherokee?" She was shocked that he knew.

"Your face and body is not that of Osage. I am Cherokee, too." GW said this in the Cherokee language.

"Your Cherokee name?" GW asked again.

"It's Ahyoka, it means..." she began to tell GW.

"She brought happiness. I know. I understand Cherokee," GW interrupted her.

For the remainder of their time, they talked about how she came to be with the Osage and how GW's family came to be Cherokee.

An hour later, the lead warrior (who Jesse met at the winter roundup camp) found them. They were taken back to the Chief's lodge. Once inside the gun belt was handed back to Jesse, and the Chief spoke.

"You are young, but you have an understanding of what must be done in order for men to come together and talk about what is needed for men to find peace amongst them. You travel with a Cherokee mixed blood, which shows us that you live what you say. You have said that these same men came into your camp to steal, and yet you called them brother. You gave us your weapons showing us that you, too, want peace with the Osage. You gave your cattle to us in times of great hunger. Let it be said that the Osage are people of peace; we will release them to you. Go in peace." Chief Bigheart gave his word that they could leave without harm.

"Thank you for showing your great wisdom on this matter. I will tell others of your wise counsel and leadership. You have shown that you, too, want peace. The Pawnee will tell their Chief of what happened here, as I will tell the Blue Coats of your actions," Jesse placed his hand over his heart to signify the sign of peace.

The lead warrior, the interpreter, GW and Jesse made their way to the center of the village. The lead warrior spoke of the decision to the village. They were cut free and told that Jesse spoke on their behalf and this was as sign of peace, never to return to the camp. The captive warrior's ponies were given back. Jesse, GW and the Pawnee rode out of the village together. About a mile out of the village Jesse stopped. It was time for his friends to say their goodbyes.

"You are free to go." He signaled that they could go home. Each Pawnee warrior came over and symbolically touched Jesse and GW on the left shoulder, yelping out a battle cry as they vanished into the thicket. Jesse was glad it was over. It could have gone badly for all of them. He knew that he overstepped his bounds and endangered GW by including him in this.

"Let's go home," GW said to Jesse.

"Let's go home," Jesse answered.

{The Taylor's arrive}
"There they are!" Alex spotted her parents stepping off onto the platform. Even though she wasn't enthusiastic about her parents coming for Jesse's sake, she was glad they were all right. Her mom reached out and hugged her, "I've missed you, and look how much you have grown."

"Dad!" Alex goes to him giving him a big hug.

"Alexandria," he said with a rigid pat on her back. She was hoping for a more loving response.

"Hello, Margaret. Good of you to meet us at the station. Where is Antonio?" Joseph asked.

"He is back at the ranch. He sends greetings and will see you when we all arrive back," Megan answered.

"You must tell us everything that has happened since the start of the summer," Mary (Alex's mom) said to Alex.

The ride back to the ranch was a short one filled with non-stop talking by the girls. Megan and the Taylors caught up on news from back East and the business of the ranch.

By the greeting her dad gave her, Alex knew he was still disconnected from her. He never had any real interest in her doings. He was all too happy to send her away to Aunt Meg's so they could be more social with their friends. She missed them when she was younger, but now she couldn't wait until it was time for them to leave. She had to find the right time before Jesse and GW came home to talk with her parents about Jesse.

Back at the ranch, Sanchez and the boys were mending the barn, getting it ready for the upcoming winter storms. Old feed and hay were being moved up down. Bags of winter feed and new hay were arriving from today's train; they were to be stored up high. Getting everything ready for the winter was priority on the ranch.

They pulled up the big house, "Hello, Antonio," Joseph called out.

"Hello, Joseph," Tony climbed down the ladder to

formally greet them.

"Hello." Mary leaned over and gave him a hug and a sisterly kiss.

"Hello. Hope your trip was a comfortable one." Tony shook Joseph's hand while he embraced Mary.

"Glad to be off that train. Much too crowded for me." Joseph preferred his privacy. Truth be known, he liked being around those of his social status instead of the working class.

"Welcome. Everyone please come in," Meg said.

Everyone went in except Joseph. He sat down in the rocking chair on the porch for a smoke, hoping that the luggage would be brought up by someone other than himself. Cody and TJ were heading toward the barn with more lumber when Joseph yelled out to them.

"Hey, you Cowboys, come and fetch our luggage," Joseph yelled out in a snooty tone as if everyone should know who he was. The boys ignored him and went on to the barn. Tony came out to see what Joseph was yelling about.

"Let us bring up your luggage." Tony slapped Joseph's shoulder as he passed. Joseph winced with pain as he rubbed it. He didn't care for

Joseph's attitude toward the boys. The boys had never seen him before today. Cowboys know what they were hired to do. Fetching luggage was not one of the jobs. Attitude was something that cowboys don't do well with.

"I can't see why they couldn't stop and bring the luggage up. They are just hired cowboys. Surely they can get out of the barn and help out," Joseph was exasperated by the way the boys ignored them.

"Maybe you'll fall into the outhouse some night," Tony said under his breath.

"What's that?" Joseph said.

"I said you missed the fall and it would be good to have the luggage in the house and get a good night's sleep."

"Ah, yes, we had a good autumn, very colorful. Yes I'm a bit tired. A good night's sleep will be good," Joseph said.

Meanwhile, on the trail home, GW and Jesse were deciding to either push on or make camp. The north wind kicked up sending a chill. It was already late afternoon. If they were to stay this night they had to find a campsite, preferably shrub covered so they can find fuel for the fire and cover from the wind.

"I'll be glad to get home and into my bed. My butt sure is sore from doing all this riding," GW said.

"I have to admit we have been pushing hard. I'm sore myself," Jesse answered.

"I have to meet Alex's parents when we get back. How's about we make camp?" Jesse suggested.

"It sounds good to me. It's not too cold of an afternoon. Better you than me meeting parents," GW looked at the sky. He didn't see any clouds that might indicate foul weather."

"I'll gather some wood and you make camp. Sounds all right with you?" Jesse asked.

"It sounds good to me. Make sure to get enough wood to last the whole night just in case the weather turns." GW didn't care to be cold.

"I think you're right about that," Jesse dismounted, took the saddle off Mariposa, and set off to gather wood.

"How does jerky and biscuits sound tonight?" GW asked.

"Sounds about right, and some coffee would be

nice," Jesse said as he left.

The Taylors were settling in. The luggage was taken up to the guest room and Sanchez back to work, spending as little time as possible with Joseph. He would have dinner with all of them tonight; in the meantime, he didn't have to listen to Joseph.

He thought to himself that it is for only a week. Surely he would be too busy to be bothered with him. It would be nice if he would just be more appreciative of his boys. They work hard and deserve to be treated with respect. They earn it each and every day.

Tony met the boys at the hay lift and lent a hand. His mind wandered and he wondered if the boys were okay. It's funny how a man gets attached to young men under his care. He treats them like men and yet he worries about them as if they were children.

"I wonder how I would have been as a father," He asked himself out loud but not loud enough so anyone could hear.

His thoughts went back to the days of his youth on the banks of the Brazos River. He tried to busy his mind so he wouldn't have to think about it. It worked for a time, but still he thought of the last night he spent with her. It was vivid reminiscence, with detailed action of the night.

"Senor Sanchez, we are crammed up here with all the hay it can hold. What do you want to do with the rest of it?" Cody yelled.

"Ah, what?" He was brought back to the present.

"Let's put those in the empty stalls. Make sure that the older bails are in front and get the new grain stored in the back of the old grain." Sanchez gave the boys direction and he went back to work. The rest of the day was spent getting the rest of the feed stored. Sanchez took some time to get the unused saddles and tack oiled and put up. The barn was getting filled with winter provisions; he needed everything in its place.

The farrier was scheduled to come in on Monday to shoe the working stock first and then cut hooves for the rest. There was a call for twenty remounts, so they would have to be shoed and broken. Several of the stalls had to be kept clear so he could bring in the horses to be shoed. The days were getting shorter with crisp air now a daily occurrence. Work days were getting shorter. It was dark when the boys began theirs and dark when the day ended.

"Okay boys, time to quit, supper is about ready

for you. I will be having supper in the big house tonight," Sanchez yelled up to TJ and Cody.

Getting cleaned up these days was done hastily. The water in the trough got cold quickly. Sanchez thought of excuses not to have dinner with the Taylors but none was sound enough to keep him from being there.

"I wish we had some of Miss Meg's roast tonight," GW said.

"I wish I had my bed tonight; this ground is getting hard," Jesse replied.

"Getting soft on me?" GW quipped back.

"Just tonight, I can just smell that roast and fresh coffee myself," Jesse said.

"Hot apple pie would be good about now," GW added.

"Look at us a bunch of homesick cowboys," They smiled and chuckled a bit.

"Got to admit, I do miss home cooking," Jesse added.

"That's not all you miss," that familiar smile was on GW's face.

"I reckon not," a smile on Jesse's face told it all.

GW added more wood to the small fire. It was going to be a cold night out on the prairie. Jesse hunkered down for the night. He pulled his hat over his face and tucked the horse hair blanket tighter around his neck. The camp was situated in a ravine with the cedars blocking most of the wind. It was a hard life being a cowboy out in the elements. A true cowboy didn't complain much as it was the life he chose.

Supper with the Taylors was pleasant. Sanchez figured they had time to rest. He called it an early evening and said his good nights. He was tired from the day's activities and needed a good night's sleep. He thought of the boys being out tonight. For a moment he thought of looking for them.

"Can't be a mama cow worrying about those two being out of sight," Sanchez called it a night and said goodnight to Meg.

"You want first watch?" GW asked.

"Sure," Jesse answered. The fire was just high enough to provide just enough warmth. They camped in a grove of Eastern Cottonwoods mixed with cedars. The wind was blowing just enough to bring a chill. Jesse thought of his family. He knew that he needed to get off another letter before the winter hit. After his family his mind went to Alex and her parents. He never met parents before. That is, he never met a girlfriend's parents. Being pre warned about her parents was even more stressful. Knowing that it was a waste of time to worry about it, he meditated on other things and tried to put this on hold until tomorrow.

"Mom, can we talk?" Alex waited until her dad went upstairs to ask.

"I think we need to. I wanted to wait until your dad went to bed, too," Mary replied.

"Alex, tell me about this Jesse." Alex knew the tone. This put her on edge knowing that her mother was going to get as much information about Jesse to be used when it suited her.

"What's his full name, dear?"

"His name is Jesse De La Souza," Alex said proudly.

"Where does his family come from, Mexico, no California?" Mary's face said it all.

"Your Aunt Meg tells me that he owns his own gear, horse, and is hard worker," And so it begins, the motherly interrogation.

"Yes, he is. His family works a ranch....," Mary interrupts Alex by asking more questions.

"So his family works for someone?" Mary needed to know if he came from family or was simply the hired help.

"No, his family owns the ranch," Alex replied.

"That is what he is telling you, so why would he be working on a ranch as a hired hand in the Oklahoma Territory if his family owns a ranch in California. It seems to me that he may not be telling you the truth. Alex, surely you didn't fall for that story, did you?" Mary was trying to create doubt in Alex's mind.

"He has no reason to be telling anyone a story. He has his reasons for being here," Alex gave her mom a stern look.

"Cowboys will say anything to get what they want, and usually from unsuspecting, young gullible girls," her mother said.

"Mother, I am quite sure that he is telling me the truth. When you meet him you can see that for yourself." Alex was beginning to lose her temper.

"So, where is this cowboy? I was hoping to meet him today," Mary continuing her inquisitorial comments

"He is gone to visit an Osage village," Alex was on to her mother's ways, she slowed down and was getting her responses under control.

"Why would anyone visit an Indian village? I think he is not here because he knows that we would see right through him. And besides, can we afford to have two cowboys absent when there is work to be done? I certainly hope we are not paying them wages for their absence. I will have to look into it."

"I bet it was his idea that he be gone when we arrived." Mary continued her interrogation.

"We didn't even know you were coming until after he told us of his plans," Alex defended Jesse.

"When do you expect him back?"

"They will be back sometime at the end of the weekend."

"He wanted to postpone going to the village until after your visit, I asked him to go so we could have a chance to talk," Alex said.

"I knew this would happen and that you would judge him before you even knew him," Alex finally said what she felt.

"I am protecting you dear; you just can't trust anyone that doesn't come from a good family. What's more, he's a man, isn't he, a Mexican cowboy, you say? They will say and do whatever it takes to get an advantage, if you know what I mean."

"You mean a family with something to add to the good name of the Taylors. You're looking for someone that can bring you more status, more wealth, more of the pretentious thing that you enjoy. Not me, I want someone who cares for me, who respects me, who makes me laugh, and someone who just gets me. I don't have to pretend around him, I can be me," Alex was clearly upset and lost her composure. Mary had won this round.

"Alex, don't be so naïve. Men want only one thing from a woman. We have to use what we have to get what we want. The sooner you understand this, the better you will be. It's time to grow up dear," Mary said.

"Mother, I'll never be like you," Alex quickly responded.

"We'll see, dear, all in good time." Mary said.

"I have good news for you. Your father wanted to tell you, but I might as well tell you tonight,"

Mary decided months ago when she received the letter from Meg telling her of the quarterly profits and of news from the ranch that she was going to enroll her in college of her choosing far away from the territory and him.

"We had to pull some strings to get you enrolled into Wilson College in Chambersburg, Pennsylvania. Only the best girls from the best families go there."

"You didn't even ask me what I wanted to do," Alex was not pleased about the news.

"You know your father. He is always looking out for your best interest. He didn't want you to worry about things. He was so happy that he could get you in. Please don't spoil his surprise," Alex was incensed about them going behind her back to decide her future. It was just like them to manipulate her life.

"I would have thought that you would be more grateful about the news and the efforts we are making to guarantee your future," Mary said, playing the quilt card.

"I would appreciate it more if you let me decide on what is best for me. I am not a child anymore. It wasn't her future they wanted to guarantee, it was their own.

"You're acting as one when you can't accept the opportunities we have provided for you."

"I'm going to bed!" Alex had had enough and had nothing more to say.

"Remember to act surprised in the morning. Don't spoil it for your father. He worked so hard to get this for you," Mary knew she had Alex. She had more experience in this sort of manipulation and questioning.

Alex stooped at the top of the stairs but decided not to say anything more. It was just like her to try to make her feel guilty for not accepting what she wanted. She wants what she wants without taking into consideration your feelings. And it is just like her to spoil someone else's news; even if it was going to be bad news. She can't keep secrets.

{Meeting the Taylors}
The day dawned with a chill when the boys started to rouse. There was a thin layer of frost on the windows. It was a strange quiet start for the boys. Sanchez had built up the fire in the fireplace earlier. The boys enjoyed a hearty breakfast of eggs, ham, bacon, and buttermilk flapjacks.

Looking out the window, Tony saw the glow of the kitchen fireplace and no other lights. It was a late start over at the big house and abnormally late start for Meg. With guests in the house they must have stayed up late. It was going to be a full day today for the three of them. With Jesse and GW back at the end of the week, they would have to work on Sunday to have things ready for the farrier on Monday.

Jesse and GW were up at first light. It was cold enough last night that they didn't sleep much. The wood gathered was barely enough to keep the fire going throughout the night. The horses were made ready; they broke camp without even having a cup of coffee.

Being too cold to carry on much of a conversation, they rode in silence. GW thoughts were on the Cherokee/Osage translator. He fancied her, and a return trip was in his future. He had asked permission to do so before he left. She was of the age to be married. He was thinking of having a family.

Jesse broke the silence. "What are you grinning about, GW?" GW had 'the cat that ate the canary' grin.

"Her name is Ahyoka. You know the interpreter," GW answered back.

"I got a notion that that's who it was." He smiled at GW.

Jess's thought went back to Alex's parents. He knew that he had to make the best impression that he could make. Knowing what he knew already, it was going to be difficult. He would have to just be himself, but be watchful on how he answers them. He had plenty of time to think about things. They were still a half day's ride out.

"Good morning, Alex," Meg was up getting breakfast started before Mary and Joseph came down.

"Care for a cup of coffee?" Meg was already pouring one for herself.

"Why do they always have to be so difficult? Yes, thank you," Alex answered back.

"Because they are your parents and they have forgotten what it was like to be young, and you're welcome."

"I don't want to go to Wilson College." Alex talked between sips.

"What are you talking about?" Meg asked.

"Did she not tell you? They have decided that I should go off to Wilson College in Pennsylvania for the fall semester. I have never mentioned anything about going to Wilson. I have my decisions made for me just like I'm a child," Alex answering between sips.

"In their eyes, you are," Megan reminded her.

"I'm 18 years old. I should know what I want to do with my life," Alex's attitude was one of displeasure.

"Well, what do you want to do with it?" Meg asked.

"I want to go to the college of my choosing and I want them to like Jesse."

"I see." Meg sat down to wait for things to finish cooking.

"And where do you want to go to college?" Meg asked.

"I was thinking I might go here. It will be easy getting enrolled here, and that way, I can still be near the ranch to help you." Alex was calming down.

"Alex, I think that you want to be near the ranch in the hopes that Jesse will stay on for a few more seasons," Megan was questioning her motives.

"Is it that obvious?" Alex said.

"You had me convinced," Meg answered as she sipped on her coffee and rolled her eyes.

"Aunt Meg, how can I get them to realize that I am old enough to decide things, and how can I make them see how Jesse makes everything seem right? My parents see only what they want to see in a person. They had already judged him without knowing him like we do."

"Maybe you shouldn't. Let them see Jesse and let them decide. Jesse will be himself, and maybe that will be enough," Meg advised.

"What if it isn't enough?" Alex sighed again.

"I'm afraid that is all we can do. You can't change your parents for who they are. Your parents will always decide what they think is best until you are independent of them. You cannot change parents' attitude about people either."

"He has been through a lot. I don't want him to get hurt from this." Alex was remembering their conversations.

"I think he will do fine. I think you underestimate him." Aunt Meg reached over and took her hand.

"He finally opened up to me right before he left. He had a lot of hurt coming from his family. I can only tell you that he came this way to get over it."

"From what I have seen, he has overcome whatever was hurting him, and you had something to do with it." Meg patted Alex hand.

"I think he did that on his own. He wants to do so much with his life. He has a plan for his life," Alex caught herself before saying too much.

"I think about him all the time." She took another sip of her already cold coffee.

"I haven't noticed," Aunt Meg said, teasing Alex as she refilled her cup.

"Be there for him if your parents don't approve of him. You know what type of person he is. I see how he looks at you. I like him," Meg placed a hand on Alex's shoulder.

They heard someone coming downstairs and quickly changed the subject. Meg got up to get breakfast ready. Alex began setting the table and got the biscuits out of the stove. Alex's parents came in and sat down without asking if they could help with anything. For most of their adult life they have been in the public service and are used to being served. Being at their sister-in-law's did not change that.

"Good morning to you," Meg greeted them.

"Good morning," Mary answered, noticeably staring at her empty cup.

"Mother, would you like some coffee?" Alex asked.

"Yes, and can you bring me some sugar and cream?" Mary said in a demanding tone to Alex.

"It's right in front of you," Alex pointed to the containers while sighing a tone of exasperation to let her mom know that she was not happy with her.

"So it is." Mary noticed the tone.

"Joseph, don't you have some good news to tell Alex this morning?" Mary doesn't miss any opportunity to get her way.

"What news?" He asked.

"You know, the good news about college," she reminded him.

"Alexandria, I do have some good news for you. I received word that you have been accepted to Wilson College in Pennsylvania. I had to call in some favors to get this done for you," Even her own father let it be known that he had gone out of his way.

"I know. Mother told me last night," Alex wanted her father to know that secrets are not kept.

"Oh well then, you should be happy that you are in good company at Wilson," Her father was rather pleased with himself.

"I don't want to go," For the first time in her life, she openly told her father what she thought. She had always wanted to tell him what she thought. It's time that they heard what she wanted to do with her life.

"What do you mean, you don't want to go?" Joseph had never been told no by Alex.

Instead of being argumentative, she decided to take a different approach. "Mother, I apologize for my rude behavior last night and for this morning. After thinking about it, I shouldn't have said those things to you. I was tired and being in my moon time I said the first thing that came into my head. You two have always had my best interest. I want to thank you for doing so."

"Well, that's more like it, and I accept your apology." Mary liked that she won out on this and now she set her mind on making sure that Jesse was no longer in the picture.

"Father, I would like for you to see that there may be another alternative to Wilson College that would save you a small fortune and still obtain the same objectives." Alex said.

"Go on." Joseph was intrigued with the possibility of saving money and still obtaining their objectives.

"It came to me last night. I think you're going to like it. It was so obvious and I am surprised that you did not think of it yourselves," Alex began to weave her plan on her unsuspecting father.

"Go on, go on," Alex had gotten her father's attention.

"Now Joseph, we have already decided that Wilson was the logical choice for her. We just can't undo what took you so long to do. It wouldn't be fair to turn our back on those who helped you get this appointment." Mary was caught off guard. Alex was attempting to manipulate her father.

"Let her finish. I'm intrigued by this. Alexandra must have had a plan all along. Let's listen to what she has to say," Joseph liked that she finally decided to speak on her own behalf instead of caving in to their decision. He finally had what he wanted from her along, strength of character.

"We can save money by my staying here at the ranch. You can pay me a salary and charge it off to the government. I will use that money to pay for college. Then you won't be out any money," Alex was not through with her plan.

Met was not sure what she was up to. This was not the Alex she knew. This Alex was manipulative, more like her parents. Meg did not like this one bit. She decided to see where she was going with this.

"I want to have the same life you have, to serve in public life. I want to serve in this territory. It will soon be a new State. I want to be part of the new State government. Then you will have contacts in the Midwest. Think of the possibilities. New land will soon open up to settlers and the prospects of new land purchased at low cost if you had someone in the know. A new State will mean new opportunities," Alex was sickened for coming up with such a story. It went against everything she knew that was right.

"Interesting," Joseph said.

"She is more than welcome to stay here while she goes to school. I can use her help," Meg caught on to what she was doing.

"I'll have to say that it is an interesting proposition. Let me study on this. I say it has some tempting possibilities," Joseph said.

"I think we should keep with our decision to have her go to Wilson," Mary wanted nothing to do with this plan. Joseph went back to eating his breakfast. The decision to table the idea of Alex going back east to school did not sit well with her. She would speak with Joseph about it later.

"Jesse where are you? I need you," Alex didn't mean to say it out load. Only Aunt Meg heard it. Meg quickly made small talk to her guest to take the attention away from Alex.

The boys were making good time. With the wind coming up, they made make-shift ear muffs from their bandanas. Both had their chaps on to help shield their legs. The open plains offer no defense from the winds. With heads low, they rode home in almost complete silence.

"We'll be home soon," Jesse turned his head slightly in GW's direction.

"I'm looking for that warm bath and some home cooking, not to mention my bed," GW answered without looking up.

{The land of fire}

Jesse wondered what his family was doing. In his mind, he went home. He saw his mother busying herself with the house hold chores along with his brothers and sisters. He saw them playing in the fields alongside the workers. He now saw them picnicking on the hillside in spring. What a vision, flowers of every color, shape and aromatic scent.

In the San Joaquin Valley seasons come and go without much warning. The springs are short, the summers long, dry and hot, very short autumns and long wet winters. The Mediterranean type climate is ideal for many varieties of food crops. You can travel up and down the State and find something ready to harvest. The land is rich and fruitful. Any conceivable plant life can grow somewhere on the land.

The coastal foothills are ideal for grapes. There's no place like it. Birds have no reason to migrate. You'd find winter snows up in the higher elevations if you wished to go there, and warm sunshine days in the southern portion of the State. Work on the ranches and farms go on year round. Production of crops goes from season to season without ceasing. The central California section of the state varies with several micro-regions, each with its own particular climate.

With spring gentle breezes come down from the Sierra Nevada. They are crisp with a hint of pine. The season brings forth the explosions of color everywhere. There is not a place where every color conceivable cannot be seen. Every inch of meadow, hillside, rocky outcrop, along stream and creeks, marshes and open range lands is covered with annual wildflower color. The Spanish Galleons visiting the coastal areas and later the inland dubbed this land, "The land of fire."

The orange poppy is the most prolific wildflower in the state. The plant is now the California state wildflower. The whites, blues, yellows, purples, reds and every other color that nature creates all bloom in the spring. California sunflowers, Pitcher sages, Pleasant Valley Mariposa and Pussy Paw lilies are abundant in the valley.

Hundreds of varieties of wildflowers are found until their peak season, which ends in mid-April. Then they disappear until the next year.

"This is looking familiar," GW broke the silence.

Jesse looked up, "sure does."

"Okay, Rose. Let's get amovin', I am beginning to smell like you," GW said to his horse.

"I have to tell you that you have smelled like that horse since we left," Jesse said.

"I have to admit, I don't know who smells worse, me or Mariposa." Jesse making fun of himself.

"I think you win out on the one," GW answered back.

It took the rest of the afternoon for the two to finally get to the ranch. Since they still had some daylight left, they found the others and chipped in where they were needed. No need to waste good daylight. All five of them worked on fixing the barn and the stable siding. GW and Jesse shared their adventure. Like a good story teller, GW added to the story, much like a fisherman. It was good to be back at the ranch. It was good to be home.

"Ok boys, time to pick up. We'll finish in the morning," Sanchez had enough. Orders from the boss said don't be late for dinner. He was not looking forward to dinner. Now that Jesse is home, most of the attention would on him. He wasn't looking toward to that either.

Being Saturday, not baths were the order of the day. GW and Jesse were in need of that and more. Taking turns since they only had one trough, it took a bit to get to everyone. The bunk house rule was that you had to have one once a week, needing it or not. Depending on what the condition was in the bunk house, you could take more. Sanchez liked his bunk house clean.

"Are you about ready Jesse?" Sanchez asked.

"Yes sir," Jesse made sure that everything was in its place.

"Can't improve on what you don't have," TJ yelled.

"No, but who is meeting the parents?" Jesse pointed out.

"Better you than me," GW's answer to anything he didn't want to do.

"Where's the hot water? Next week someone else gets in last," It wasn't Cody if he didn't have something to complain about.

"Okay, okay, let's go. Don't want to keep them waiting. Good thing you two come home early. I didn't want to make small talk tonight. Tonight it's about you," Sanchez was in a good mood.

"It wasn't enough that I have to make an impression, but I have to talk to them. What do I say to them?" Jesse asked.

"Let them talk," Sanchez answered.

"They love to talk about themselves. You have to be mindful of what you say. Mrs. Taylor will keep a record of what you say. One word of caution here, I wouldn't mention a thing about the times you spent with Alex."

"Why?" Jesse asked.

"She wants to humiliate you in front of Alex and make what you two have inappropriate. Don't give her reason to," said Sanchez.

"Just be yourself. We all know you. They do not. If you get upset, don't let them see it. She wants nothing better than to put you in your place," Sanchez was poking Jesse on the chest.

"What does that mean?" Jesse asked.

"Jesse, all that means is that she thinks you are not good enough and is looking for the opportunity to show everyone, especially Alex, you are not good enough for her."

"Ready?" Sanchez wanted to stop all the questioning so the evening could start.

"Not really, but I'll have to be" Jesse held his head high and chest out.

"You want to keep seeing Alex?" Sanchez said it more as a statement than a question.

"Yes," Jesse missed the meaning.

"Then be yourself. You have only one chance to make a first impression," Sanchez opened the door and led Jesse out.

The big house was lit as if it was Christmas. The wrap-around porch had all the lanterns on. Looking through the window, they saw every light downstairs lit; both fireplaces with fire, which made for a cozy setting. The dining room table was set.

"Good, I see that you brought the bottle of wine," Sanchez made sure that Jesse didn't come empty handed. He wanted Jesse to have everything he need for proper etiquette when meeting the Taylors.

Sanchez knocked on the door and waited until someone came to answer instead of walking in as he always did. It was Meg. She hugged both and whispered in Jesse's ear that she was happy that he and GW were home safe. Jesse saw Alex coming toward them from the corner of his eye.

"Why did you knock? Look at you two, all dressed up, I should have these dinners more often," Meg loved embarrassing them.

"Hi, I was going to say something to you when you rode in, but you two went right to work. I'm glad you're home." Alex wanted to hug Jesse but thought it was not in their best interest to do so in front of her parents.

"I thought it was best if we helped out since we were gone. I need to tell you about what happened. Oh, I brought this for tonight. It is bad manners not to bring something to dinner," Jesse handed Alex the bottle of wine.

"Hey, it's only us." Alex said.

"I assume these are your parents coming toward us?" Jesse stopped talking and stood just a bit taller.

"Are you going to introduce us, Alexandria?" Mary came into the living room from the kitchen.

"Yes, of course. Jesse De La Souza, may I present my parents, Mr. and Mrs. Joseph Taylor of Virginia."

"How do you do, Mr. and Mrs. Taylor," Jesse firmly shook Mr. Taylor's hand, keeping eye contact. Mary held out her hand to see what he would do. As with formal introductions, he lightly kissed her hand and then took a step back. She was looking for signs to indicate his lack of social graces.

"Alexandria tells us that you come all the way from California? Is it as wild and uncivilized as they say? No wonder, with all those Indians and Mexicans still thinking that it is still Mexico." Joseph looked around laughing, as if he made a clever remark.

"Yes, I hear the uncivilized are heading that way from the east," Jesse answered with a snappish tone making sure that he still had eye contact. Sanchez cleared his throat to get Jesse's attention and as a reminder to Jesse as to whom he was addressing and to get his tone under control. He was there to make a good impression no matter what the Taylor's views were on the West.

Wasting no time, Mary asked, "Why are you here if, your family owns a ranch?" Alex gave her mother that I can't believe you just asked that look.

Jesse knew it was the beginning of a long evening. He answered, "Being ranchers, we sometimes need to find a new way to improve our productivity so that our net profits will increase. After all, that is why we are in the business. I am here to find out how business is done in the Oklahoma Territory. Your ranch came highly recommended. I am honored to be working here learning your methods. If the United States government trusts you, then hopefully, I can benefit from your expertise."

"We can't argue with that. Our bottom line is healthy. Come tell us about your home," Joseph loved flattery and was looking for more.

"Mary asked, "Why do you work as a hired cowboy. Would it be simpler if you just asked how we do things?

"No ma'am, my father requires us to work the ranch. It is not enough that we understand the business. We have to have working experience. Knowledge is one thing, but working experience is more valuable. One truly doesn't know the business of ranching unless he actually gets his hands dirty and understands all the working of ranch life," Jesse directed this to the Taylor's lack of work experience. Mary Taylor caught the insinuation.

"Dinner is served," Meg said as she came in the save Jesse.

Everyone made their way to the dining table. Jesse waited to see if Mr. Taylor offered his wife a chair. He did not. He sat as if he were the guest of honor. Jesse looked at Sanchez. Tony knew what he was thinking and slightly shook his head to tell him not to say anything.

"May I?" Jesse pulled out the chair and waited until Mrs. Taylor sat down and then he went over to Alex and did the same. Sanchez did the same to Meg, and then they sat themselves.

"Thank you, Jesse," Mrs. Taylor was gracious in the gesture, impressed with his thoughtfulness, but she was there for a reason, no matter how mannerly he was. He would never be good enough for her plans.

"Yes, thank you," Alex said after he seated her.

"Shall we say grace? Megan asked Sanchez. Joseph began saying grace, arrogantly, he thought it was his table to do so.

The evening continued, with Joseph wanting to be the center of attention and Mary wanting to know particulars about Jesse. Alex was on edge with questions directed to Jesse by her mother and Jesse answering as tactfully as he could. Meg and Tony were trying to redirect Mary's attention away from Jesse most of the evening. Somehow they all survived the evening.

"Good night. Jesse and I have to cut our evening short tonight, some of us have to work in the morning," Sanchez announced.

"The night is just starting. Surely you can stay?"

Joseph liked the attention he was receiving from Jesse.

"We would like to but ranch work is never done, and our day starts early. Thanks again for the evening, Meg. Good evening," Sanchez motioned Jesse to leave with him.

"Mr. and Mrs. Taylor, it was good to finally meet you," Jesse made the proper gesture. When the two finished with their goodbyes, they walked to the stable to check on the horses. Jesse didn't say a word. Sanchez wanted to know if he was okay. With Jesse not wanting to talk, he took it that he was handling it.

"Good night, son," Sanchez patted Jesse on the shoulder.

"Good night, sir," Jesse had his mind on other things.

Sanchez went back to the bunk house and stayed up a bit longer. He poured himself some coffee, lit his pipe and rocked in front of the fireplace, pondering the evening. Cody, GW and TJ were playing poker. A typical night in the cabin.

Sundays were usually off days, but the winter was setting in and they had to catch up before the first storm. With all them back, it would not take a whole day to do so. Monday the furriers were coming and all had to be ready for them. Everyone did what was needed without much talk. It was getting cold.

With the furrier's work complete, Jesse spent most of his time working away from the ranch. Sanchez thought it best if the boys took some time helping nearby ranches since their work was caught up and it was the right thing to do. In doing so Jesse wouldn't have to be around to visit with the Taylors. Sanchez knew that Mary was not going to let up until she found something to use for her purpose.

In the West, neighbors helped a neighbor and that was how it was. No payment was necessary; just a hand shake and a thank you was all that was needed. Sometimes a pie would be given. Who could say no to a freshly baked pie? If it was late in the afternoon when the work was done, a meal was provided. A neighbor helping a neighbor was the cowboy way.

Some stray cattle were rounded up and taken to the Osage village, even though it had only been a short time since they were there. Sanchez thought it would be a good gesture if the cattle were given before the storms hit. The boys were greeted in the village as friends. This time they stayed for a time to get acquainted with the

people. The last time it was a tense situation.
This time they were openly welcomed by all.

GW spent most of his time visiting with Ahyoka.
Their intentions were made known to Chief
Bigheart. GW had to have his permission to do
so since she was part of the Chief's family they
headed home before the winter storms hit,
promising to come again. GW would be back
whenever he had a chance to.

They Taylor's left the ranch with unanswered
questions about Jesse and where Alex was going
to college. Alex was happy to see them leave so
everybody could loosen up. She knew that Jesse
avoided them so they would not ask any more
questions. She was ready to see him and have
their time together. She needed to be with him.
She missed his kiss.

The remainder of the winter was routine. The
winter was not particularly a cold one or one
with much snow. The worst days came in
February and early March with ice storms. The
life on a ranch during the winter was one of
survival for the livestock. The cowboys were
always on the lookout for stress from the stock.
It was their life and they were happy for the life.
Anyone can put on a cowboy hat and say they
are a cowboy. It has nothing to do with a hat,
it's the lifestyle that makes one a cowboy.

The winter gave Jesse and Alex more together time. No subject was off limits. He was so comfortable being around her. Her parents didn't enter their minds throughout the winter and spring months. The big house was always occupied by the cowboys. The big house was home to the young men. Meg loved this time. She got to know each one. They were her children. She loved them all.

{The telegraph from Padre Diego}

To Jesse De La Souza, Lee Ranch, Valley of the Still Waters, Oklahoma Territory. Stop... Come home immediately your father has taken ill. Stop... It is influenza, he asks for you. Stop.... Take the train home immediately. Stop.... I am waiting for your reply. Stop.... Padre Diego. Reply: To Padre Diego, Our Lady of Mercy. Stop... I will leave Still Waters immediately. Jesse. Stop.

"I have to leave on the next train. My father has taken ill. I will return when I can, Mrs. Lee," Jesse found Mrs. Lee to explain his going back home.

"You just don't worry about that. Be safe. We want you to come back when you can. Jesse, we all want you to stay with us permanently if you want to. Did you tell everyone?" Meg hugged him.

"I've told Senor Sanchez and the boys. Thank you. I would like to stay on. I need to find Alex to tell her that I'm leaving," Jesse appreciated the offer.

"There you are," Jesse found her in the stable grooming Sam.

"I wanted to see you before I left," Jesse approached her with his hand held out.

"I heard you were leaving. Are you coming back?" Alex asked. She had her head down.

"I'm leaving Mariposa here, can you watch over her?" Jesse asked.

"So you really are coming back?" Alex was relieved.

"I said that I am coming back. I just can't leave my horse and not come back," Jesse answer was not taken as it was intended. Alex was looking for another reason from him.

"Is that all you're coming back for?" Alex looked down again.

"No," Jesse grinned and moved closer to her.

Alex threw her arms around him, and without

saying a word they stayed embraced for some time. Jesse explained that he had to go home because his father had taken ill. This would hopefully be a good time that he and his father could mend their relationship. Jesse had forgiven him and he wanted him to know this in person before it was too late. They talked about her parents and made plans for Missouri to visit Sam and his family. He had planned to stay another season and wanted to know how she felt about it before he asked Mrs. Lee. This was the decision she wanted to hear from him. She was pleased.

{Homecoming at the Madre De la Tierra Ranch}

There was no one waiting for him at the station. Jesse picked up his luggage and walked home thinking that it was odd that no one came to the station to pick him. The ranch was a way off so it took him a while to get home. When he got closer to the ranch he saw a large crowd of people in the courtyard. There was no mention of a gathering. Then he saw the faces of those gathered, grief stricken faces. The crowd recognized Jesse and parted as he made his way to the bedroom. His family was inside along with Padre Diego. He was too late. His father had passed an hour before he arrived at the station. His mother hugged him and said that he asked for him before he passed.

"I tried to get here as soon as I could."

"He had asked for you numerous times. He wanted to tell you that he was sorry for the things he said," his mother embracing him even closer.

"I too wanted to tell him that I was sorry for what I did. I had forgiven him for the things that he had done and needed for him to hear it from me. I needed for him to forgive me," Jesse missed his opportunity to say the things that he needed to say.

"He had." His mother kissed him on the forehead. The rest of the evening was spent visiting with family and friends who came to pay their respects. Stories were shared.

"How are you?" Jesse asked his mom when the last of the guests left.

"I'll be fine, Jesse," Her face said otherwise.

"He wants you to take over the ranch," his mother revealed to Jesse.

"Why me, I have a life back in Oklahoma," Jesse thought went to Alex.

"You are the oldest. He wanted the responsibilities of the ranch passed down to you," Jesse's mother letting go of him.

"What about the Tios? They know the ranch. The men will respect them."

"No, it must be passed down to the eldest son. It must be you. Hijo, su familia necesita usted ahora. (Son, your family needs you now.)"

The rest of the night the family made the necessary plans for the service and burial. Carlos was to be laid to rest in the Cypress grove next to the vineyard where he spent most of his free time. With the service over, the burial was a private one with only the family present. Padre Diego said all the things that Carlos would have wanted him to. His headstone faced the vineyard and the Sierra Nevada. He was buried at the very site where he stood every night watching the vineyard. Padre Diego confided in Jesse telling him that his father spent hours looking toward Mariposa. Carlos hoped that he would see Jesse's return. He needed his son to come home, and he wanted to rebuild a relationship with his son.

"Jesse, he truly wanted to change after you left. Carlos came to mass more often with the family. He was so proud of his son in the way he defended the family and how he stood up for what he believed was right. Carlos said that you had courage beyond your years," Father Diego embraced Jesse.

"I was too late to let him know that I forgave him and I needed for him to tell me that I was forgiven," Jesse said.

"He knew. I read your letters to him. He missed you. He changed from the man you knew, becoming kinder, more appreciative of what he had. His family meant more to him than all his possessions."

Jesse spent the next few weeks with his family telling them of his adventures. He spent the nights pondering his decision about what to do about what to do about the ranch. He knew his mother was right; it was the responsibility of the oldest to take over. Any other time he would not even question it, but he had his life back in Oklahoma and Alex to think about. His head was saying one thing, but his heart was saying another.

He looked for Lee, only to find out that the family had moved to San Francisco a year ago when the rail project was completed in the Valley. During this time, the Chinese immigration to the United States was being stopped. The expulsion of thousands of Chinese was taking place. Violence increased. Jesse sent a telegraph looking for the where about of the Sheo family. His contacts in San Francisco telegraphed back saying that they were there for a while but were deported up to Oregon. He feared that harm had come to them.

His decision would have been an easy one if he was back in Oklahoma, but he was not. His decision was not just for himself anymore, he had his immediate family to consider. He did what he always did when he had difficult decisions to make. He sought counsel with Padre Diego. He made his way to church.

"Padre, are you here?" With hat in hand, he entered the church.

"Always here for you," Padre Diego was coming out from behind a curtain and greeted Jesse.

"What troubles you?" Padre Diego asked, although he knew from Juanita why Jesse came to see him.

"I have a difficult decision to make. I don't know what to do. Whatever I decide, it will end up hurting those that I love. My head and heart are not as one."

"What does your head and heart tells you, Jesse?"

"My head is telling that I need to take over the responsibilities of the ranch, and my heart is telling me to go back to Oklahoma and be with Alex."

"You can do both, take over the ranch for your family and see if Alex would want to come out here."

"She has her heart in going to a university back east. I, too, want to go to the university."

"You can attend a university in California and still run the ranch. Your Tios will run the ranch while you are away. If it were meant to be, she will attend the university back east, and when she is finished, if she still feels the same, she can visit the ranch and you two can decide what to do from there."

"But her family is back in Oklahoma and Virginia," Jesse answers back with added emotion.

"And yours is here," Padre Diego answers Jesse back with the same emotion.

"I want her to be family someday."

"If you two truly want to be together, you will work it out."

"I want it to work out. I need it to work out," Jesse said.

"Jesse, your family needs you," Padre Diego pointed out that family responsibilities fall on the eldest.

"I need Alex in my life, too."

"Go back and see if you two can come up with a plan that the both of you can live with."

"What if she doesn't want to come out here after she graduates?"
"Then you will have your answer," Father Diego stated the obvious.

The last two weeks were emotionally draining for Jesse. Jesse buried his father without saying what he needed to say. His anger prevented him from saying the words that maybe could have healed the relationship between them. Never would he leave without saying the things that needed to be said.

Jesse boarded the train after telling family and friends he would write back as soon as he could. He had unfinished business back in Oklahoma. Padre Diego was to visit the family while he was away. Jesse left the day-to-day running of the ranch to his uncles, which was the logical choice at the time. The inheritance papers that were drawn up by the attorneys were not signed. For the time being, the ranch was still in his father's name.

He telegraphed Alex to tell her that he was on his way home. He didn't say anything about the decision he had to make or the passing of his father. He thought it best to visit with her face-to-face. There was something that he needed Alex to hear in person, and he wanted to hear her answer in person.

He wrote to his mom to let her know about how difficult this decision was going to be. He talked about the Oklahoma family. He wrote about what Alex meant to him and how he looked up to Senor Sanchez. He gave more in-depth information about Senor Sanchez. He wrote about how he wished his father and he could have had a relationship like he and Senor Sanchez had. He felt guilty for wishing that Senor Sanchez could have been his father. He told of his riding partner, George Washington Smith, and how he wanted GW to join him in his ventures after he left the Lee Ranch. If he chose to take over the ranch, he wanted GW to come back with him and stay at the ranch.

{Home at the Lee Ranch}
Alex was already at the station waiting for Jesse. She had been waiting for over an hour. The train was late because it lost time when it picked up passengers in Guthrie. It didn't matter how late it came in, Jesse was coming home. He was on

the forward passengers' car and was one of the last ones off. He caught Alex by surprise by walking up on her from behind. Alex surprised him by wrapping her arms around him and squeezing him so hard that he almost lost his footing on the ice.

"I've missed you," Alex said over and over again.

"I've missed you more," This was Jesse's standard reply.

"If it's okay with you, I've made reservations at the cafe for dinner. I wanted you to myself before you got to the ranch." Alex knew that everyone would want to visit with him as soon as he got home.

"Perfect. I have time to see everyone else later." Jesse was so happy to be home.

It didn't take too long to get to the cafe since the station was at the end of town. Every available table was taken. Alex managed to secure a booth so they could have a little seclusion. She had paid for the reservation earlier to make sure they had a place to talk.

"So, how are you?" Alex wanted to know how his visit was.

"Alex, I have difficult decisions to make," Jesse's

indicated that they were serious in nature.

"Are they about me?" Alex was fearful that it was bad news.

"The decisions I have to make do concern you and my family. I've said that I would always tell you everything, and this involves you. First of all, I was too late, my father died before I got home."

"I'm sorry," Alex took hold of Jesse's hands.

"I didn't get to tell him what I needed to say. My mother said that he was sorry for what he had done and forgave me for leaving. Padre Diego said that my father knew that I had forgiven him and how I wanted him to forgive me," He paused for a minute before he spoke again.

"I have to decide whether to accept my inheritance or pass it to my little brother. The problem is that he is too young to take on the responsibilities. My uncles would have to take the ranch until he grows up."

"What do you want to do?" She was thinking that because of her he had to choose one or the other.

"That depends of what you want to do?" He was looking to see how she reacted.

"I can't be a part of this decision," she said.

"You said that you always wanted to own a ranch and have a vineyard. You have that now."

"I want to go to a university to study too, but that would be difficult if I have to run things," Jesse said.

"I'm sure you can do both if you work it out with your family."

"Perhaps," He said.

"I want you to be a part of my life, Alex."

"I know you do. But I have my dream of going to the university, too," she said.

"And I want you to go, and after you graduate we can be together." Jesse interrupted her by pulling her hands closer to him. There was a moment of silence between them.

"What are you asking me, Jesse?"

"I'm saying that I need you in my life. I love you. I'm saying that I want to marry you."

"Are you sure you know what you're asking? Have you thought this through?"

"Yes, more than I ever wanted anything," Jesse said.

"I have only one answer," said Alex. Yes, Yes, Yes!

"That was what I wanted to hear. How about we order some dinner? I'm starving" as they hugged, the dinner crowd applauded, which embarrassed them both.

"Alex, I don't have a ring at the moment. I wanted to make sure that we were on the same page."

"That's okay, we can get one later, and I don't need a ring to tell me how you feel. The love we share is all I need, I gave you my heart long ago."

"I'll write and tell my family of our decision. Are you going to write yours?" Jesse motioned the waiter that they were ready to order.

"Yes, as soon as I can." Alex thought about what had just happened and now she had to tell her parents about what they decided. It was not going to be easy, knowing how they felt about Jesse. Jesse was a strong-minded young man and it didn't matter to him how her parents felt about him. The rest of the time was spent talking about this trip home. The evening went well except for the lingering thought of how she was going to tell her parents. She needed to talk to Aunt Meg about keeping this quiet until she found the right time to tell them.

"Welcome home!" Meg yelled from the front porch.

"It's good to be home," Jesse answered while approaching Meg with arms looking for her motherly hug.

"Come in and tell us about your trip," Meg gave him a welcome home hug and kisses on both cheeks.

"I would like to, but I've been traveling all day, and it's getting late," Jesse said.

"I understand. How about tomorrow, we can have lunch here?" Meg asked.

"Okay, good night then," Jesse needed to talk to Sanchez.

"Good night," Meg gave him another hug. She missed him as if he were her own son.

"I have something to tell you," Alex said to Meg.

"What is it? Did he bring you back something

from California?" Meg was ever curious.

"Yes, he did, but that's not the surprise," Alex grinned from ear-to-ear.

"Okay, out with it already," Meg couldn't stand the suspense.

"We are getting married when I graduate!" Alex shouted.

"What?" Meg was so happy about the news. She held up Alex's hand to take a look of her ring.

"I'm so happy for you both. So where is it?"

"I don't want you to say anything to anyone. I don't know how to tell my parents, or if I should until I graduate. Oh, he hasn't gotten it yet."

"It's a long time before you two get married. The right thing to do is to tell them. But I see your point," Meg added.

Meg asked, "How do you feel about it?"

Alex responded, "No words."

"Have you thought about what your parents would say to this? Your parents won't approve of this marriage."

"I know. I want this more than anything," Alex said in a melancholy tone.

"Well, you have a lot of time to think about it." Meg hugged her once more.

"Yes, I do. What do you think?" She valued Aunt Meg's advice.

"I love you both and want the two of you to be happy, but I see that there will be complications."

"I'm happy about my decision, but I have some reservations, too. You are right; You're always right. I need to think about this more. Good night, Aunt Meg," she embraced her.

"Good night, dear. Pray about it. I find it best when we involve our God," Aunt Meg kissed her on the forehead.

"Remember, not a soul," Alex smiled at Aunt Meg and bounced up the stairs to her room, but not to sleep. She contemplates on how she was going to tell her parents. Alex slipped into bed without turning on the lights. She loved the idea of being married to Jesse and she wanted all her family to accept him. She wanted her children to be accepted by her parents. She wanted Jesse to be happy. Why does life have to be so complicated? Her heart wanted this more than anything. Her head was saying, "Think this through."

"Hey, you made it back!" Sanchez said, shaking hands with Jesse. The others did the same.

"I missed all this snow," Jesse jokingly responded.

"I think he missed something else," TJ said.

"For once, you are right," Jesse answered.

"Hey, partner," GW came over and shook hands with Jesse.

"Well....," TJ was waiting to hear about this trip home.

"Bittersweet," Jesse said.

"What does that mean?" Cody asked.

"It was good to see my family, but I arrived too late. My father passed before I got there."

"Sorry," Cody said. The others patted Jesse on the shoulder.

"Bad deal," GW placed his hand on Jesse's shoulder, too.

"Thanks everyone. I appreciate your words. Can I talk with you in private? Jesse asked Sanchez.

"Sure," Sanchez motioned that they go outside to visit.

They walked out of the bunkhouse to the stables. Jesse wanted to see Mariposa and it would be more private in the stables. The walk over was quiet. He looked in the direction of the big house and saw that Alex's lights were not on.

"Senor Sanchez, I have to make decisions that are going to change my life."

"Go on."

"With my father's death, I inherited the ranch."

"And so, what is the decision you have to make? Sanchez lit his pipe.

"I can either go home and run the ranch or leave it to my younger brother."

"Why you are having trouble making this decision?"

"I don't want to leave here. I like it here," Jesse looked up to Alex's room.

"That may be so, but I think there is more to this." Sanchez knew the reason. He wanted Jesse to say it.

"Yes, sir, there is more. I don't want to leave Alex behind."

"I see. What does Alex have to say about this?"

"She wants what I want. We laid out a plan for her to meet me in California after she graduates from the university."

"She has agreed to your plan?" Sanchez was surprised of the plan.

"Yes. I basically asked her to marry me when she graduates. I'll visit her whenever I can during the school year."

"Basically, there is no basically here. Either you did or didn't," Sanchez wanted to make sure that Jesse knew what he had did.

"I did ask her, and she has accepted," knowing what he knew about how the Taylors felt about Jesse, he needed to have Jesse understand what he was up against. The Taylors would not welcome him into their family. Alex's life is not her own. Her parents were constantly interfering in her life. Money or the lack of money has a way of influencing your choices.

Parents in their best or worst intentions usually live through their children. Reasons for manipulating their children lives may be due to a discontented life or unrealized dreams of their own. It is their children who have to bear the hurt of decisions made for them. Hindsight is the reason for two of the most painful works spoken, "What if." He felt he had to say something to Jesse. He did not want him to go through the same pain as he did.

"You have to make these decisions on your own. No one can make them for you. A ranch is what you wanted to have, so you could grow your vineyard. Your family needs you, and you need Alex. As far as I can see, you consider all things. Above all, follow your heart. Don't have the 'what ifs' in your life if you can help it." The two walked back to the bunk house. Sanchez lit his pipe yet again, rocking in front of the fire stoking it. Jesse sat in the rocker next to him drinking coffee, chewing on a bacon and biscuit sandwich and contemplating his future.

GW, Cody, and TJ continued playing cards while chewing on strips of bacon as if they were cigarettes. The dogs begged for any scraps of food. The boys gave each dog a piece of bacon. Satisfied, the two curled up in front of the fire, content, and fell asleep. Soon, they all called it a night and went to bed.

The rest of the winter was spent making sure that the remounts were ready to be shipped to the forts in western Oklahoma Territory along with their ration of beef. It wasn't too harsh of a winter, so it was a relatively maintenance free time.

With the decision to marry after graduation, Jesse sent letters to tell of their decision. A letter was sent to Sam explaining his reason for not finishing his travels east to visit. He explained that he would do that when he could bring his wife.

Another one was sent home to tell his mother that he would accept the inheritance and would be back at spring's end. He had to finish the job in Oklahoma before he headed home. With their plans laid out, he now could leave, knowing that his future with Alex was intact. The thought of having a wife made him think of the responsibilities he would have. A responsibility he would gladly accept. Two years would not be that long, he thought.

{Jesse leaves to go home}
With the spring roundup over, the conclusion of the boys' work year was complete. Everyone was asked if they wanted to stay on. Cody, GW, and TJ agreed. Jesse was going home and GW

would follow him as soon as he and Ahyoka were married.

Alex was packed and ready to go back to Virginia to be with her parents before she left for school. She decided to accept her parents' proposal to go to Wilson College in Pennsylvania. She still had not told her parents about her engagement. She found it better to not tell them until she graduated.

Alex said her goodbyes to the boys as they came into the stable to fetch their horses. With hugs all around they exchanged words and more hugs and then they went to their assigned jobs for the day. Senor Sanchez knew this routine as she had said goodbye to him since she was a child and always she came back as he knew she would the next summer.

With everything said and goodbyes taken care of, it was time for her to meet the morning train to head east. Aunt Meg and Alex had said their goodbyes before she went to the barn. Jesse brought up the wagon and loaded their bags. He drove her to the station to see her off, with Mariposa in tow.

"It is difficult to watch you leave, Alex."

"It won't be long before we can see each other again, Jesse." Alex was beginning to tear up.

"I'll visit whenever I can," Jesse promised her.

"I know you will. I'll write, and you do the same. I have your address, and I will give you mine as soon as I'm settled."

They could see the train coming from miles off. It wouldn't be much longer and she would be off. Alex nervously checked to make sure she had her ticket and money. Keeping Jesse close, she held his hand, wishing that she had more time to be with him. As the train pulled in, she stood even closer to him. She waited until she was the last one to board. She kissed him and told him that she loved him, and boarded the train. The taste of her kiss and her scent were forever etched in his mind. She took a window seat so she could see him. As the train pulled out, she opened her window and called his name.

"Jesse, I love you!" Waving her goodbyes from the open window.

Jesse stayed on the platform until he could no longer see the train. His heart was breaking; it was a hurt that he had never felt before. Tears filled his eyes and his throat hurt. He tried to keep it in, but the pain was too great. His train headed the opposite direction an hour later. He watched Mariposa being boarded, went to her and gave her a treat, and talked to her before he boarded himself. Sanchez rode up to take the wagon back. He shook Jess's hand and told him that he would be missed by all.

"Goodbye son. Remember what we talked about. I'll be seeing you later," They hugged. It was getting to be all too much for Jesse. He was already missing his Oklahoma family. The trip home was a long one. He wrote several letters, one to Mrs. Lee thanking her for treating him as family, one to Sanchez for listening to him and treating him as a son, one to GW thanking him for being his friend and reminding him that he was to come out and be part of the family, and one to Alex telling her that she was the love of his life and the one who filled his heart.

When the train stopped to pick up more passengers he mailed the letters. Days later, he was met by his family at the Merced station. He was prepared to take over the family ranch, knowing that everything was taken care of in Oklahoma. First he sent his luggage home with his family, and then he waited for Mariposa to be taken out of her car. He had to do something before he went home.

He rode first to the church to find Padre Diego. He couldn't locate him. He knelt at the altar and thanked God for watching over him and for letting good things come into his life. He prayed for all those in Oklahoma, and then he left to do one more thing before he went home.

Arriving at the Cypress grove, he stood in front of his father's grave. He said that he was home. He was ready to take over the responsibilities now. He left home to find himself. He found the one above all and he found love. He discovered many things about himself and that you cannot rely on just yourself. You always have someone watching over you. You need your friends, and most of all, you need to have your family. Money cannot buy happiness. Happiness comes from within and having loving relationships. He stayed at the grave site visiting with his father and saying what was in her heart. He didn't want to leave anything unsaid.

His first night home was one filled with relatives coming over for dinner. The night was a long once with friends and family coming by. It was good to be home with family. The next morning, he met with the attorney and signed the inheritance paper. The ownership was transferred to Jesse. The first order of business was to meet with his uncles. He sought their wisdom and thoughts about how the ranch could be ran more efficiently. He wanted their input. They were a big part of his plan. He wanted them to know that they are the ranch as much as he was.

{Arriving at Wilson College}

With Alexandria going to Wilson, Mrs. Taylor had gotten her way and was pleased with herself. What she didn't know was that she was oblivious to Alex's plans. What Alex didn't know was that her mom was ahead of her in this game.

With the Taylors' influence at the college, Mary Taylor had one last strategy make sure there was no contact between her and Jesse. Mary knew that she had to take matter in hand. She needed inside help.

"Joseph, will you wait here? I have to visit with Mrs. Dunn to make sure that Alex is taken care of." Mary reached into her purse to make sure she had what she needed.

"I thought we had taken care of all her needs already?" asked.

"I wanted to make sure, that all. It won't take long." She walked into her office without knocking.

"Mrs. Taylor, come in. What can I do for you?" Knowing the likes of the Taylors, she knew she was up to something.

Mrs. Dunn, as headmaster at Wilson, I am assured that you will comply with my wishes." She handed her the envelope.

"Yes, of course, Mrs. Taylor. You and your husband are among our finest contributors to our college. What is it that you wish from us?" Mrs. Dunn would do anything to continue receiving funds from the Taylors.

"I need Alexandria to focus on her academics without distractions. You know how young ladies' minds are easily preoccupied with thoughts of young men."

"Say no more. I will make certain that she is engaged at all times," Mrs. Dunn added the name of Alexandria Taylor to her ledger where other girls' names of prominent contributors were listed.

"I would like for you to make certain that she does not receive any correspondence from young men, nor do I want her to correspond with them. Do you understand what I need done?"

"I understand. I will take care of it personally. You have nothing to worry about. I do this for other girls as well. We need to have our young ladies minds focused at all times," Mrs. Dunn had kept mail from leaving or being received from students per parents' requests.

"Very good I will leave it in your hands," Mrs. Taylor closed her purse and had her plans in motion.

"Will we be seeing you and your husband at dinner tonight? You are seated at my table," Miss Dunn asked.

"We will be attending." Mary turned and walked out.

"Joseph, our business is concluded here," She walks ahead of him.

"What did you do?" Joseph grabs her arm from behind.

"What any good mother would do to protect her child from making a mistake," Mary walked ahead of her husband knowing that she had the last say.

{Reconnecting twenty-five years later}
"Do you think he'll recognize me?" Alex looked in the mirror.

"I look old." Alex was looking in the mirror.

"You look beautiful!" Aunt Meg yelled from the kitchen.

"You're just saying that because you're my aunt."

"I say it because it's true. Now go pick him up.

He'll arrive around noon if it's on time." Meg was getting things ready before everyone came.

"How did you ever find him?" Alex stopped at the door to make sure that she didn't forget anything.

"It took a while for the operator to find him. Then she made the call for me. I spoke to his sister. I like having this telephone. It was hard to understand her, but I managed to get my message across," Meg was getting the last of the refreshments ready.

"I never received any letter from him. All I can figure was that he changed his mind and forgot about me," Alex said as she primped at the mirror.

"Why don't you ask him when you pick him up?"

"Okay, I'm leaving, I'm taking the automobile," Alex looked one last time in the mirror and shrugged her shoulders.

"Try not to run into anyone this time," Meg reminded Alex of the last time she used the automobile.

"I saw Mr. Wilson at the post office and he told me his leg is doing much better, so watch out for people crossing the street. Now please hurry, he will be coming in soon," Meg pushed her out the door.

"I had one little accident...," She mumbled under her breath. She arrived at the station without hitting anything or anyone. With so many coming off the train at one time it was not easy to see if he came off. She was sure that she would recognize him. Maybe he didn't recognize her and went on to the ranch. What if he wasn't on the train at all? She was walking away and heading to the end of the platform when a familiar voice stopped her.

"Hello, Alex. You still have that walk of yours."

She stopped and turned around. It was one of those moments when time stands still. She closed her eyes as she turned. Was it really him or was it her imagination? She opened them and he appeared, much older, but it was him. He had the same smile, the same eyes. It really was him.

"You look as beautiful as the last time I saw you," Jesse stared into her eyes.

"Hello Jesse. I believe it was right here. I was leaving to go home," She kept her eyes on him, still not believing it was him.

"Can I hug you?" He asked.

She held her arms out to invite him in. Tears of happiness filled her eyes. She didn't want to let him go. He had remained in her heart all these years. Without even a thought she kissed him deeply. The old feelings were there. Kissing him was like she remembered. She still loved him. He embraced her, remembering how good it was to hold her. The warmth of her body filled him with memories of being together. She was in his heart. Jesse kissed her back. The taste of her kiss was the same.

He whispered, "I missed you."

Alex responded in kind, "I missed you more."

"Alex, what happened? Why did you not write back? I wrote you for so long and heard nothing from you." Jesse held her arms with tears forming at the corners of his eyes.

"Jesse, I wrote you every week and never got a response. I even went as far as to telegraph you. I still did not get a response. Did you change your mind about me?" Alex was tearing up as well.

"I never received a telegraph from you," Jesse responded.

"How could we write each other and never

receive any of it?" Alex was starting to think that something was wrong with all this.

"You know I remember the first week in college the headmaster insisted that I bring all my correspondences to her. In fact, there were several girls who were asked to bring all their correspondences to her. I received mail from my friends and parents." Alex thought for a bit more.

"I received mail from the ranch," Jesse added.

"Do you think that your parents had something to do with us not getting our mail?" Jesse was trying to find a logical answer.

"Mother couldn't be that devious."

"All I know is that I had no word from you. I thought you had changed your mind, so I went on. Alex, you never were out of my thoughts." Jesse looked down at her ring finger. He saw what he hoped he wouldn't see.

"I think we need to go. They are expecting us," said Jesse, abruptly changing the subject.

"Yes, you're right," Alex felt his nervousness.

"Are you okay?" She asked.

"Yes, no, I should not have kissed you like that. I don't want anyone to say anything to your husband."

"Oh, my ring," Alex looked down at her ring finger.

"Jesse, I moved on, too."

"I can see that."

"He passed five years ago. He was a Navy captain. He contracted a respiratory disease in the Orient and died at sea. He was buried at sea. I never got to see him."

"I'm sorry."

"He was a good man," Alex said.

"Did you have children?" Jesse wanted to know more.

"We could never have children."

"How about you, did you marry? Have any children of your own?"

"No, I never did marry. After my mother passed, I spent most of my time running the ranch and traveling. I never saw the need to," he didn't want to tell her that he was heartbroken when he heard nothing from her.

"Was there someone special?" She asked.

"There was someone once, but it didn't work out."

"What happened?" She asked.

"She didn't like cows." They both got a laugh at that. Jesse picked up his bag and they walked off the platform. Alex pointed to the automobile and got in. The ride home was an experience. Alex driving skills were something to watch and not necessarily experienced. Jesse held on and waited until the ride was over.

"Your room is ready upstairs," Alex said as the automobile came to a stop.

Jesse looked around, recalling when he was a cowboy on the ranch. The ranch was different, yet familiar. The ranch had been modernized since he last saw it. He walked to the bunkhouse with Alex following. He opened the door. The bunkhouse was empty. The mattresses were rolled and the chairs up on the table. Jesse's mind filled with memories of time spend here. Memories of the boys' playing cards and cutting up. The late night talks with Sanchez, the rocking chairs and the smell of his pipe next to the fire.

"Alex, I had happy times here," he said, turning to her.

"Did you keep up with the other boys when you left?" She asked.

"The only one I kept up with was GW."

"How is he?"

"About a year after I left he made his way west with his new wife. They came to work on our ranch. He married the girl who helped interpret for us when we visited the Osage. He is a foreman for us. He is my best friend. I'm glad he came.

"Did you ever go visit Sam?"

"I never did, but we wrote on occasions. He has a wife, two boys and a girl. He took over his parents' farm. He is doing well."

"Aunt Meg is anxious to see you. Let's not keep her waiting any longer." Alex knew what this meant to her having him back at the ranch.

Meg waited for them on the porch. With her hands over her mouth and tears running down her face, she embraced him. He knew her grief. He wished that he could have come at more happy time.

It was early autumn. The leaves had changed from the color of growth to the harvest colors of the season. It was the most beautiful time of the year, Jesse thought. The funeral was set for two o'clock the next day. The site of the burial was at the one place that both he and Alex knew well, Brush Creek falls.

After dinner, he and Alex drove out to Brush Creek. It was a drive filled with memories. There is a road where there was once a horse trail. The trees were larger. The bamboo and cattails were overgrown. The once visible cave opening was now scarcely visible. It had rained up north and the creek which fed the waterfall was flowing. The volume of the water coming over the falls was just right.

With the colors of autumn combined with the gently swaying trees, the waterfall was picturesque. The sound of the water cascading into the clear pool below added to the tranquility of the setting. The sound of water had always comforted Jesse. What a perfect place.

"I can see why he chose this place." Jesse said out loud.

"I know why he chose this place," Alex answered.

"Why?" Jesse asked.

"He wrote of it to Meg right before he passed. He wrote all of us separate letters. Jesse you have one too."

"I do?"

"His attorney gave them to us. He has yours."

"What does it say?"

"I don't know. The attorney said that you were to receive yours after the service. Tony wanted that way."

"Why did he want to be buried here?" Jesse asked.

"He owned this land and 160 acres surrounding this site."

"I never knew that." In all his talks with Sanchez, he never mentioned it.

"I didn't know it, either," Alex added.

"I'll go into town and see about the letter." Jesse was curious about what the letter said.

"If you can wait, the attorney will attend the

burial. You can get it then."

"Okay, I guess I can wait."

"Let's go home. It has been a long day for us all." Alex was exhausted. It had been an emotional week for her, and now Jesse was home. She knew that she wouldn't sleep knowing that he was in the same house.

"Yes, it has" Jesse was drained from the train ride and from the emotional stress. But being tired wouldn't keep him from staying up to visit with Alex.

He dreamt of seeing her for twenty-five years. She was very much a part of his heart. He still loved her and wanted to tell her. He didn't want to leave and have things left unsaid. Being back at the ranch, and especially at the Blue Hole, filled his heart with joy. She was so close, and for most of the time they were there, he stared at her. He didn't really hear her. He wanted to soak in the sight of her face, her eyes. Being at the big house was special. He had spent many nights taking her home and kissing her goodnight at the front door. He excused himself early and went upstairs to bed. He lay awake, thinking of the kiss at the station. It was like no time had passed. His heart ached for what could have been. He wondered if she felt the same.

Sometime during the night, Alex came in and lay next to him. Not a word was spoken. No words were needed. She laid her head on his chest and held his hand. The rhythmic heating of his heart along with the rising and falling of his chest slowly intoxicated her. She so missed him. The kiss at the station awakened her desires for him. His kiss was the same. Her heart missed him and now he was next to her.

He was dreaming, and then the dream became reality. She was next to him holding him. He lay on his back, not wanting to disturb the dream. When the dream took his hand and placed it on her, he responded. He turned to face her, and using his fingers, he meticulously outlined her face and body. Her kiss made it even more sensuous. He remembered her taste. They were one. The honesty, the trust, and the ease at which they loved each other made it seem as though no time had passed between them. The twilight passed to dawn and found them still wanting more.

{Saying Good bye to Tony Sanchez}
Everyone gathered around the final resting place for Anthony Sanchez. Tony wanted a Catholic priest to preside over the service. He was specific as to what he wanted said. The words spoken were written by Tony to his ranch family. He spoke of the love he felt for all and how the ranch was home. He spoke of Megan, Alex, and

Jesse being his family. It was like him to write his final words. These were the last words he wrote:

Before we were ever born our stories began; they will continue even when our name on the stone fades from lack of remembrance.

The priest ended gravesite mass with the reciting of Psalm 23:
The Lord is my shepherd: I shall not want.
He maketh me to lie down in green pastures: he leadeth me beside the **still waters...** As the priest recited, Jesse thought of the words. He first heard them from Father Diego at the time when he was lost. He recited those words throughout his life, and yes, they comforted him. He feared no evil for his Lord was with him during his hour of need. His journey brought him to the Still Waters of Oklahoma.

"Mr. Jesse De La Souza." A gentleman approached Jesse.

"Yes."

"My name is Calvin Johns. I have a letter and some papers for you to sign. Mr. Sanchez was very specific that you sign these papers."

"What are they?" Jesse asked.

The papers are self-explanatory. Leave them

with me before you leave town," he shook Jesse's hand and tipped his hat to Alex.

"I will get to it before I leave," Jesse opened the letter marked personal.

"Thank you and I'm sorry for your loss," Mr. Johns walked away after making his condolences to Meg and Alex.

"Did you get your letter?" Alex came up to Jesse but stayed a few steps back, not wanting to look on his private message from Sanchez.

"I just received it. Why are you staying back?" Jesse asked.

"I wanted you to have your privacy."

"You know you can read this. I have no secrets from you."

As he fully opened his letter, he saw two other letters inside. They were from his mother to Sanchez. He had no idea that she knew him other than what he had told her.

"Alex, there are two letters from my mom to Sanchez."

"Did your mom know Sanchez?" Alex asked.

"How could she? I'm about to find out," Jesse read the letter Sanchez left him first.

Jesse, if you are reading this, you're home in Oklahoma. You have questions, no doubt. The letters from your mom were sent to me after you left to go home. Your mom and I knew each other when we were both young and living in Waco. It took a while, but your mother put things together and finally wrote to me, hoping that I was the same person she knew back in Waco. We wrote and she finally told me who you were to me. I've always known that you were familiar to me in so many ways. You have a lot of your mother in you and I saw some of me in you. If you haven't figured it out, Jesse, you are my son.

"Jesse, did you have any idea?" Alex said with her hand over her mouth in surprise.

"No, my mother never told me anything. She had time to tell me, but never did. Sanchez didn't even say anything."

"He didn't even know about it until you left," Alex reminded him.

"Why would she not say anything to me?"

"What else does it say?" Alex's curiosity was getting the better of her.

Let me tell you the rest of the story so you won't have to wonder as to the whys of all this. Your father and your grandfather came to an

agreement, and it was decided that she marry him without her even having a say in it. It was the way things were done. When she found out about the marriage, we decided that we would leave together. We made plans to meet that night to go west. Her mother found out and sent your grandfather to me instead. I had to go without her in fear of my family being homeless. Your grandfather owned the house and farm that my family worked. I decided that I should go east to the Indian Nations.

"So it was my mother that he always talked about leaving behind. It must have been difficult for him all those years. I often wondered why he always told me to follow my heart," he thought back to past conversations he and Sanchez had.

"He told me stories of her but never said her name. He told me the same thing," Alex recalled her conversations with Sanchez, also.

Don't blame your mother for not telling you. She didn't know it, either, until you were home again. It was difficult for her to not tell you. Your father was your father. She didn't want to take that away since you two forgave each other. Your father never knew her secret. Fate just brought you and me together. I'm glad that we got the opportunity to know each other even, if it was just friends. Like I said before, we had a special connection. Thank you for opening up to me. It meant a great deal to me that you did. So now you know.

Now, for the other matter I want you to

**have this special place you and Alex shared along
with the surrounding land. Tell Alex that I knew
about the petrified remains in the cave. I
discovered them long ago when I first arrived. I
worked and saved my money so I could buy the
land to preserve them. I planted trees along with
the bamboo to hide the entrance. I loved this
place, which is why I wanted to be buried here. I
wanted my headstone to face the waterfall as it
was where I came to when I was troubled. Follow
your heart, son.**

"Alex, I never knew," Jesse folded the letter and
placed it in his suit pocket.

"Who did?" Alex shrugged her shoulders.

"Alex, we need to talk."

"Ok, what about?"

"Let's walk." Jesse took her by the hand as he
often did on their walks. The two took familiar
path through the Burr Oaks leading down a
ravine while visiting about the past. At some
point, they accept what happened, and to some
extent, were at peace with it. It still hurt all the
same.

"Alex, all I ever wanted was for someone to love
me as I loved them," he started and didn't stop
until he said everything he wanted to. He wasn't
going to leave anything unsaid.

"I know," she replied, pressing her hand into his. They spent hours talking about their lives. It was getting late in the day. It was time for them to get back and make their way back to the falls. Once back, Jesse looked around one last time.

"Alex, I almost forgot. I have something for you."

"What is it?"

"Close your eyes and give me your hand." Jesse reached into his coat pocket and handed Alex something that he had held on to ever since they first met.

"Okay, you can open them."

"You've kept it all these years!" Jesse had taken the pebble he found on their first date at the Blue Hole and made a pendant of it. He wore it the entire time that he was away from her.

"Whenever I was lonely or sad I took it out, and it always brought a smile to me. It always reminded me of our first date and my time in Oklahoma." They walked around the pool area, making sure those things in their hearts were said. They made the most of their time.

{Years later, 1950}
"Mr. Johnson, you are a hard person to keep up

with." Mr. Long, the realtor, walked up the bank to the pond.

"I wanted to get a good look of the lay of the land before I made my final decision."

"I noticed that this particular piece of land has bamboo. Why would anybody plant bamboo? It's such a nuisance of a plant."

"If you say so Mr. Johnson, if you could sign these papers, I can file them in the Payne County Assessor's office before it closes today," Mr. Long was trying to hand the documents to Mr.' Johnson.

"What can you tell me about his property, Mr. Long?" Mr. Johnson ignored the paperwork.

"It's right here on the deed. Before statehood, it was owned in partnership by Joseph Taylor and Tom Lee by special permission of the US. Government. It says here that Tom Lee was the operating partner. After his death, the partnership was passed down to his wife Margaret by special permission of the government. Then it changed hands to Alexandria Thomas. A year later, her name changed to Alexandria De La Souza. Her husband did not sign the deed. The last name on the deed is the current owner, Mr. C.W. Smith, who purchased the place in '31."

"Do you know the history of this area, Mr. Long?"

"I believe it was a cavalry remounting station for the U.S. Cavalry stationed in the Oklahoma Indian Territory. Then it was a wheat farm. In the late twenties, the land lay fallow. Mr. C.W. Smith bought the land and began operating dairy farm during the depression, and ran it until he retired."

Mr. Johnson walked up the embankment and went to where the bamboo was. Looking around, he noticed the depression where an exceptionally deep pool once was. The sides and bottom were rock, not dirt. The falls no longer spilled over as the creek upstream was diverted years ago.

"It looks like it was once a deep pond." Walking toward the tree line, he noticed five headstones facing the dry pond.

"What can you tell me about these?"

"I had no idea that they were even here, Mr. Johnson."
Cutting the weeds around the headstones, he read the names:

Antonio Sanchez, Born 1858, Died 1916
Tom Lee, Born 1858, died 1893

Margaret Morgan Lee (Meg), Born 1860, Died 1920
Sarah Lee, Born 1887, Died 1892
Jesse De La Souza, Born 1873, Died 1930
Alexandria De La Souza, Born 1874, Died 1931

"I wonder why they were buried here. Why would anyone want to be buried up here near this bamboo infested dry quarry? Do you think Mr. Smith knows anything about these?"

"We can ask."

"Where is he?" Mr. Johnson asked.

"He lives in the nursing home in town."

"Okay, I've seen enough. I'm ready to sign, Mr. Long," Mr. Johnson signed the documents and handed them back to Mr. Long.

"Shall we go visit Mr. Smith, Mr. Johnson?"

"Why not, since we are in town we might as well see if he knows anything about these headstones."

"I'll make the arrangements, Mr. Johnson."

Mr. Johnson made one last walk around the area and spotted the small opening to the cave from behind the bamboo. Thinking that it must have been a fox's den, he thought nothing more of it. He also noticed an opening barely large enough for someone to go into just under the lip. He looked at the direction of the headstones again, and something shiny caught his attention.

"What's this?" Mr. Johnson inspected the silver chained pendant. He turned the pendant over and saw the semblance of the little girl smiling and wondered why anyone would leave it here. He placed the pendant back on the headstone with Jesse's name on it.

"Okay, let's go, Mr. Long."

Arriving at the nursing home, they asked where they could find Mr. C.W. Smith. The nurse said that he was in the courtyard with several friends. It was his 72nd birthday party.

"Mr. Smith, my name is Dale Long."

"Yes sir," CW had on his cowboy hat.

"Mr. Smith, I am here with Mr. Johnson. He just purchased your farm."

"Can you tell us more about the people who are buried on the property next to the bamboo groove?"

"Yes sir. When I was about 18, I came to work for Mrs. Lee. You might as well pull up a chair. It's a long story, but a good one." He took a drink of his Coke and began to tell the story of when he was a young cowboy on the Lee's Ranch. A Vaquero named Jesse came from the west and changed his life........

Characters:

Jesse De La Souza -
Young man who leaves California and his family
to find himself.

Alexandria (Alex) Taylor-
Jesse's love interest

Mrs. Margaret (Megan) Lee-
Alex's aunt, owner/operator of the Lee Ranch

Senor Antonio J. Sanchez-
Ranch foreman

The Taylor's, Mary and Joseph-
Alexandria's parents co-owners of the Lee Ranch

Juanita and Carlos De La Souza-
Jesse's parents

Ging Sheo-
Over seer of the Chinese railroad work force
(CCR)

Lee Sheo-
Jesse's best friendship

Padre Juan Diego
Head Catholic priest, Our Lady of Mercy

Cody Williams

George Washington Smith (GW)
Travis John Johnson (TJ)
Ranch hands at the Lee's Ranch

Sam Jones-
Jesse's childhood best friend from Missouri

Mariposa- Jesse's horse

Ahyoka-Osage girl; GW's love interest

Acknowledgments

To my shadows, Lacey and Colton:

Story time was a treasured end to our nightly routine. No matter how long our day was or how exhausting it was, we always made time for the two of you. Whether it was a story from a favorite book or made up stories, the joy shared in this time was like no other.

Lace you knew the stories by memory and any deviations from them you would always made me start over. You never tired of them even after the hundredth time. Colton you always would say "Do the voices." We spent many nights sleeping on the trundle bed the three of us telling family stories. The most blissful time of my life was spent doing this. You two are loved. I hope you continue this with your children. We read stories and we would tell stories but the best stories we ever told were the ones of family. Being a very private person, I chose not to tell of my childhood until you were able to fully grasp them.

The quote at the start of this story is about telling family history to our children. We as parents have the responsibility to share these stories. The good and the bad, it is who we are. Our love ones who passed will not be forgotten as long as we let their stories be known to the next generation. I want to sincerely thank those who were placed in my path throughout my life. Without family, teachers, coaches, friends, and special individuals, I would never have had a story to tell or share.

To my very enthusiastic and dear friends, without them this book would not have been published. I want to thank Jennie Ross for finding such exceptional individuals to help see this project to the end. Without her tireless work in pushing us to move this project onward, it would still be on the shelf in my closet. Now for the technical help I received from those from Tennessee. I want to thank Debra Ross Patterson for her outstanding editing. I wrote like a science teacher, that I am, she made it possible for others to easily read it. I want to thank Warren Patterson for teaching me the art of fly fishing, which by the way, I'm desperately in need of more lessons. Thank you both for welcoming me into your home.

I want to acknowledge Chad Johnson for his kind words in writing my biography. I consider my wrestlers as part of my family. Chad became more than that, he is considered to be a son to me. The last and certainly not the least is Andy Mullins we could not have finished the project without your talent in designing the cover. It was a great surprise that you became a part of this project. You are a talented man. Thank you for coming back into my life. Andy was also a former wrestler. I cannot possibly thank you all enough.

If you look deeply into the palm of your hands, you will see your parents, and all the generations of your ancestors. All of them are alive in this moment. Each is present in your body. You are a continuation of each of these people.

Tich Nhat Hanh

Roger A. Roberts grew up in California's central valley during the late 50's, 60's and early 70's. Life in Merced gave him appreciation for nature, hard work, and genuine kindness and struggle. While in Merced, he could always depend on his best friend Charles Shelton and his family to insure a proper family environment and guidance along with his coach, Steve Sanchez, who shaped his unrelenting work ethic, incredible athletic ability and laser focus to develop one of the nation's toughest fighters into a magically talented wrestler showcased as a technical guru by NCAA and freestyle wrestling community. Roger Roberts was one of Merced's golden boys who made it out of the daily battles of life in the projects moving east to Stillwater, Oklahoma where he attended Oklahoma State university on a full wrestling scholarship.

While Roger was not exempt from learning some of life's hard lessons about maturity and priorities, he always had a knack for learning fast and picking the right mentors. His life in Stillwater allowed him to cross path and connect with coaching legends Tommy Chesbro and Myron Roderick.. Both of these men had a tremendous impact on his life and development into the man he is today. Under them he learned how to teach and coach and, most importantly, the true meanings of accountability, responsibility and obligation. Lessons he would pay forward later to those he coached and mentored. His days as an active Cowboy wrestler provided him with many successes as well as a few memorable failures. Those failures, he would later admit, shaped him the most. One of the greatest pieces of advice he will give is "struggle is good for you." Roger credits coaching with helping him come out of his shell, "I learned to speak more and coaching taught me to communicate with the athletes; I was kind of reclusive when I was younger." He always said it was his teachers and coaches who saved him and game him his love for learning because of the way they taught and impacted his life.

Coach Roberts has been a student of life and all of its lessons, which served as his motivation to focus on science and biology for his degree from O-State (BS Biological Science). Teaching wasn't his first choice for a career. He wanted to be an oceanographer, but there was only one class in Marine Biology at OSU. After graduation from OSU in 1978, he served as a Graduate Assistant Coach on the Cowboy squad until he departed in 1979 for the next chapter of his life, teaching and coaching in Owasso, Oklahoma.

From 1979 until 2000, Roger coached and taught in the Owasso School District. His style of coaching and teaching came from Steve Sanchez but he says he truly learned how to coach and teach while traveling with Coach Chesbro to camps and clinics during his days as a college wrestler. Although he honed his technical skills, he really learned the psychology of coaching and how each athlete/student receives and processes information differently. This served as the foundation to his philosophy that you treat all of your athletes/students the same but you can't teach or coach them the same.

After he left Owasso in 2000, Roger went to Broken Arrow School for 2 years then to Union High school for a year. He experienced several consecutive years of success during this time and decided he was ready to retire from his days as an educator. He then went back to Stillwater to start a business as contractor building homes. RCH Custom Homes was a success until the economy sent the home market into a tailspin and sent Roberts back to teaching. He continued to embrace his own advice, "struggle is good for you." Roger never turned away from his responsibilities nor did he shun his obligations. He stayed accountable throughout this period and never neglected his commitments. Coach Roberts truly lived his mantra as a "do as you do coach."

In 2010 Roger was entertaining a private school teaching and coaching opportunity in Ft. Worth, Texas. It was also during this time that he received a call about a teaching opportunity in Tecumseh, Oklahoma. Within a week of hearing about the Tecumseh opportunity, he accepted a position teaching Biology at the Central Oklahoma Juvenile Center (COJC) and has been there ever since.

In May 2012, the head wrestling coach position at Tecumseh High School became available and it was natural fit for Tecumseh to look internally to Coach Roberts. His daughter Lacey and son Colton really encouraged him to pursue the opportunity because they knew it would be good for him. "They saw how I was when I was coaching and the passion I had for it. They grew up in the wrestling room with me."

Coach Roberts still mentors and teaches his former athletes and students. He knows their families, their history, their struggles and their celebrations. He is "Grandpa" to their children and will always be the example of how to live and conduct your life. He is still the first one to arrive and the last one to leave. We can hear him now, "Oh, did that hurt? I don't feel it. Suffer in silence and get back to work. Struggle is good for you."

www.ingramcontent.com/pod-product-compliance
Lightning Source LLC
Chambersburg PA
CBHW070805180626
46818CB00001B/117